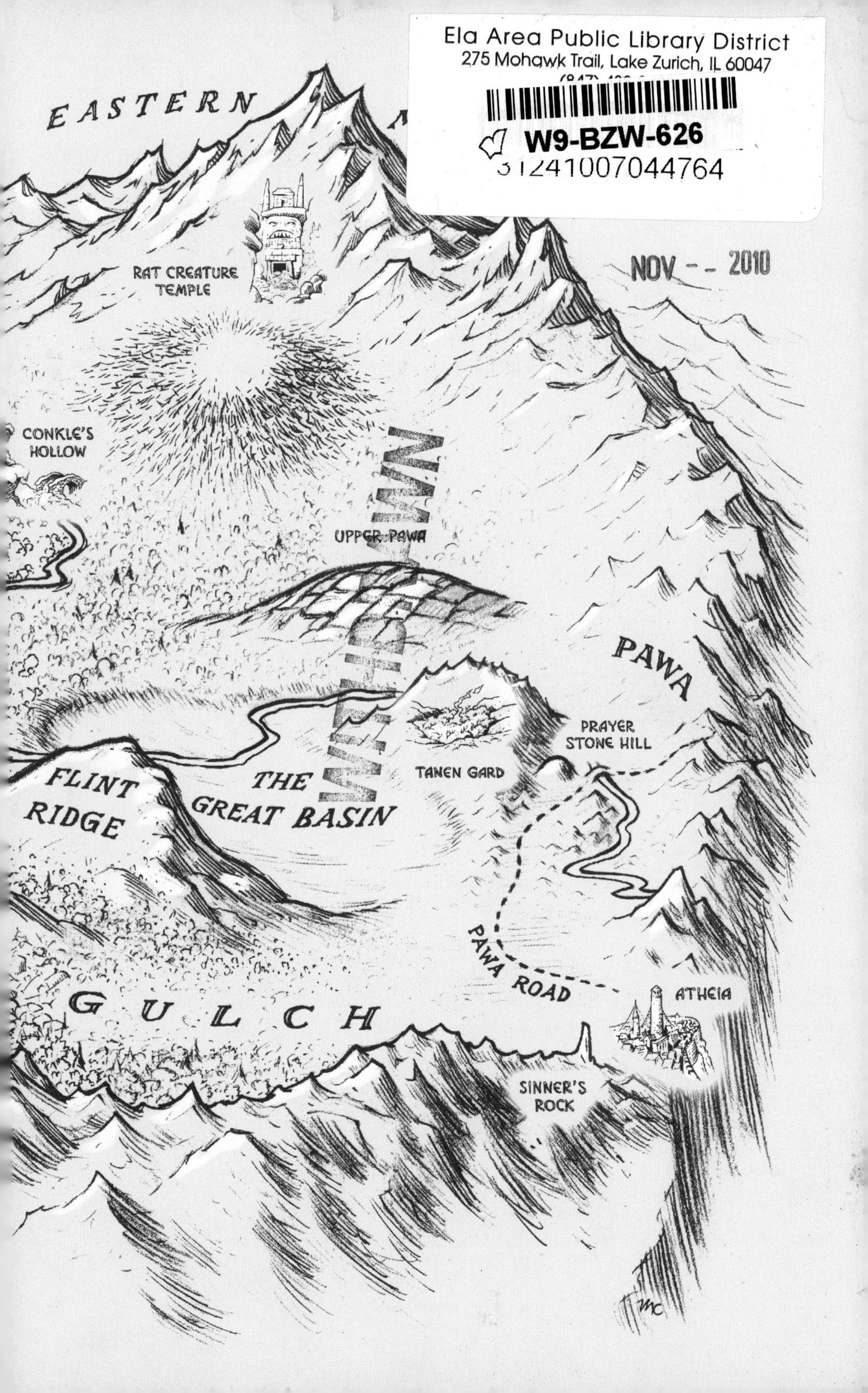
EASTERN
RAT CREATURE TEMPLE
CONKLE'S HOLLOW
UPPER PAWA
PAWA
PRAYER STONE HILL
TANEN GARD
FLINT RIDGE
THE GREAT BASIN
PAWA ROAD
ATHEIA
GULCH
SINNER'S ROCK
MC

Dreaming of Harvestar

ACCLAIM FOR JEFF SMITH'S

Named an all-time top ten graphic novel by **Time** *magazine.*

"As sweeping as the 'Lord of the Rings' cycle, but much funnier." —*Andrew Arnold,* **Time.com**

★*"This is first-class kid lit: exciting, funny, scary, and resonant enough that it will stick with readers for a long time."* —**Publishers Weekly,** *starred review*

"One of the best kids' comics ever." —**Vibe** *magazine*

"**BONE** *is storytelling at its best, full of endearing, flawed characters whose adventures run the gamut from hilarious whimsy . . . to thrilling drama."*
—**Entertainment Weekly**

"[This] sprawling, mythic comic is spectacular."
—**SPIN** *magazine*

"Jeff Smith's cartoons are irresistible. Every gorgeous sweep of his brush speaks volumes."
—*Frank Miller, creator of* **Sin City**

"Jeff Smith can pace a joke better than almost anyone in comics." —*Neil Gaiman, author of* Coraline

"I love BONE! BONE *is great!"*
—*Matt Groening, creator of* The Simpsons

"Every one of the zillion characters has a unique set of personality traits and flaws and dreams that are developed amid the pandemonium."
—*Kyle Baker,* Plastic Man *cartoonist*

"BONE *moves from brash humor to gripping adventure in a single panel."* —ALA Booklist

"BONE *is a comic-book sensation. . . . [It] is a classic of writer-artist craftsmanship not to be missed."*
—Comics Buyer's Guide

OTHER ***BONE*** BOOKS

Out from Boneville

The Great Cow Race

Eyes of the Storm

The Dragonslayer

Rock Jaw: Master of the Eastern Border

Old Man's Cave

BONE

Ghost Circles

By Jeff Smith

with color by Steve Hamaker

graphix

An Imprint of

SCHOLASTIC

New York Toronto London Auckland Sydney Mexico City New Delhi Hong Kong Buenos Aires

Library of Congress Catalog Card Number 9568403.
ISBN-13 978-0-439-70629-2 — ISBN-10 0-439-70629-7 (hardcover)
ISBN 0-439-70634-3 (paperback)

ACKNOWLEDGMENTS
Harvestar Family Crest designed by Charles Vess
Map of *The Valley* by Mark Crilley
Color by Steve Hamaker

10 9 8 7 6 10
First Scholastic edition, February 2008
Book design by David Saylor
Printed in Singapore 46

This book is for Charles Vess

CONTENTS

BONE
HEY, JONATHAN!

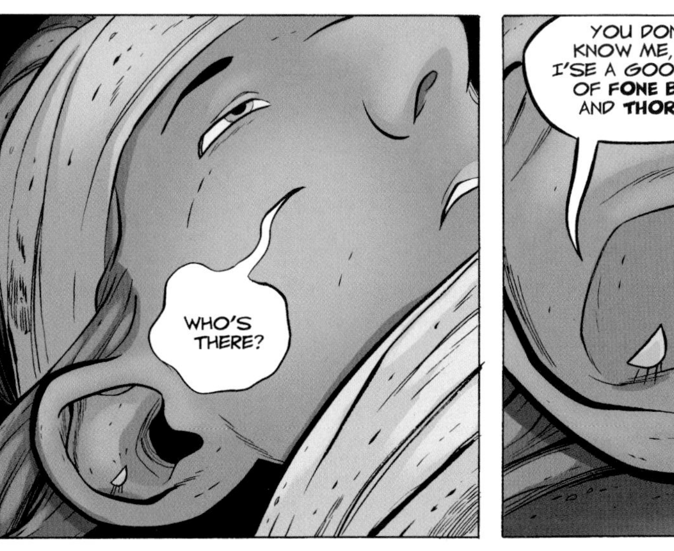
WHO'S THERE?
YOU DON'T KNOW ME, BUT I'SE A GOOD FREN' OF **FONE BONE** AND **THORN'S.**
HOW'S YOU **DOIN'?**

NOT TOO GOOD.
I'SE REAL SORRY TO HEAR THAT. THORN WILL BE, TOO.
LISTEN, JON - - THORN SENT ME AHEAD TO FIND GRAN'MA BEN AN' THE DRAGONS - - TO TELL 'EM THAT THORN'S COMIN' TO JOIN 'EM.
BUT JON - - I CAN'T FIND NO DRAGONS - - I CAN'T FIND NO GRAN'MA BENS! AN' I THOUGHT THORNY'D BE HERE BY NOW.
WHERE IS EVERYBODY?
THE DRAGONS . . . HAVE GONE UNDERGROUND FOR GOOD. GRAN'MA SAID SO.
FOR GOOD? OH, I KNEW WE SHOULDA COME BACK SOONER! I TOLD THAT GIRL, BUT SHE WOULDN'T LISTEN!
OH, BOY. . . IF THEM DRAGONS GONE DOWN INTO TANEN GARD, THAT'S A SURE SIGN THE END TIMES IS NEAR.
I GOT TO FIND GRAN'MA BEN! OR LUCIUS! YOU KNOW WHERE LUCIUS IS, JONNY?
THEY DISAPPEARED. EVERYBODY SAYS LUCIUS DONE IT.
DONE WHAT?

THEY SAY HE DONE SOMETHIN' TO GRAN'MA BEN AN' PHONEY BONE.
THAT'S RIDICULOUS! WHY WOULD HE DO ANYTHING TO THEM?
I DON'T KNOW! BUT I SAW HIM IN THE ARMS OF THE HOODED ONE - - AND SHE WAS A WOMAN! THE TWO OF 'EM JUST STOOD THERE AN' WATCHED WHILE THE RAT CREATURES SNUCK UP AND AMBUSHED OUR REGIMENT.
I COULDN'T UNDERSTAND WHY HE'D DO THAT...
I TOLD THE HEADMASTER ABOUT IT, AN' HE SAID LUCIUS WAS A TRAITOR! I JUST...
HE'S MY HERO.
NOW, SON, HE'S NO TRAITOR. THERE'S A EXPLANATION, YOU CAN COUNT ON IT!
I HOPE SO...
LUCIUS DOWN IS A HERO. AN' A MORE LOYAL SOUL I NEVER MET. ESPECIALLY WHEN IT COMES TO GRAN'MA BEN!
WHY, WHEN OL' ROSE BEN HAD TO PICK UP STAKES AN' MOVE TO THE NORTHERN END OF THE VALLEY, LUCIUS COME WITH HER, JUST TO MAKE SURE SHE AND HER GRANDDAUGHTER WAS SAFE!
ARE YOU SURE?
DON'T YOU WORRY NONE. IF THEY'S ANY HUMAN BEING YOU CAN COUNT ON, IT'S LUCIUS DOWN. I PROMISE YOU THAT.

DO YOU THINK LUCIUS WILL FORGIVE ME FOR TELLING THE HEADMASTER . . . ?
OH, YEAH. DON'T WORRY, YOU DONE THE RIGHT THING. LUCIUS WOULD BE PROUD OF YOU.
YOU GONNA BE OKAY?
I WILL NOW.
OKEE-DOKEE, JONNY BOY! I'LL FIND OL' LUCIUS, AN' YOU REST UP, 'CAUSE YOUR REGIMENT GONNA NEED YOU REAL SOON.

Ghost Circles

BONE
WENDELL!
SIR.
SIR!
THE HEADMASTER REQUESTS YOUR PRESENCE ON THE MAIN GATE.
MM?
OH, YES, OF COURSE. HAS SOMETHING HAPPENED?
I BELIEVE THE SITUATION HAS BECOME WORSE.
PLEASE HURRY.

WORSE? WHAT DO YOU MEAN?
THE EARTH TREMORS.
. . .THE HEADMASTER FEARS THE END MAY BE COMING.
THIS WAY PLEASE. HE IS WAITING FOR YOU.
YOU SENT FOR ME?
YES, TINSMITH. YOU ARE LUCIUS DOWN'S BEST FRIEND, CORRECT?
WELL, COMMANDER DOWN AND THE QUEEN ARE MISSING.
THEY HAVE BEEN MISSING SINCE EARLY TODAY, AND WE ARE HOPING YOU CAN SHED SOME LIGHT ON THEIR DISAPPEARANCE.
I'M HIS BEST FRIEND? I THOUGHT HE WAS ONE OF YOU - -
. . .VENI YAN MONKS.

I BELIEVE YOU WERE GOING TO SAY STICK-EATERS.
WE KNOW HOW YOU FEEL ABOUT OUR ORDER, TINSMITH.
BUT YOU ARE WRONG ABOUT LUCIUS DOWN. HE WAS NEVER ONE OF US.
HE FELT THAT OUR ORDER'S OATH OF LOYALTY CONFLICTED WITH HIS DUTIES...
...WHICH, AS CAPTAIN OF THE GUARD, WAS TO PROTECT THE ROYAL FAMILY.
AND AS YOU KNOW, EVEN IN THE OLD DAYS, LUCIUS WAS PASSIONATELY LOYAL TO THE TWO PRINCESSES BRIAR AND ROSE.
HE ALWAYS WAS SWEET ON OLD ROSE BEN, I KNOW THAT.
YES, WELL ... AT BEST, HIS ALLEGIANCES ARE FOGGY.
I UNDERSTAND THE DISAPPEARANCE OF COMMANDER DOWN AND QUEEN ROSE MAY BE LINKED TO ONE OF THE BONE CREATURES... THE ONE WITH THE STAR ON HIS SHIRT.
PHONEY BONE! YES, SIR! THE RAT CREATURES WANT HIM! THAT'S WHY THEY'VE SURROUNDED US! THAT'S WHY WE'RE AT WAR!
THIS WHOLE THING IS PHONEY BONE'S FAULT!
DO YOU KNOW WHY THE MONSTERS WANT HIM?
SOMETHING ABOUT THE STAR ON HIS SHIRT.
"THE ONE WHO BEARS THE STAR."
LOOK OUT THERE, TINSMITH. DO YOU SEE THE LEGIONS OF OUR ENEMIES CAMPED AT OUR DOORSTEP? DO YOU REALLY BELIEVE THEY'VE COME HERE FOR ONE OF THE RIDICULOUS BONES?

WHAT ARE YOU TALKING ABOUT?
TELL ME, TINSMITH, HAVE YOU EVER SEEN ONE OF THESE BEFORE?
UH . . .
HAS THE KINGDOM BEEN GONE SO LONG THAT YOU NO LONGER EVEN RECOGNIZE THE ROYAL SEAL? THE HARVESTAR FAMILY CREST?
THE CREST!
IT HAS A STAR ON IT.
WHICH REPRESENTS THE DREAMING. . . THE SOURCE OF LIFE ITSELF.
OLD ROSE BEN AND HER GRANDDAUGHTER THORN ARE THE CURRENT KEEPERS OF THE SOURCE.
THEY HAVE SECRETS THAT COULD HELP THE RAT CREATURES FREE OUR OLDEST ENEMY . . .
THERE . . . IMPRISONED UNDER THAT SMOKING MOUNTAIN LIES THE LORD OF THE LOCUSTS.
LORD OF THE LOCUSTS? YOU DON'T EXPECT MY VILLAGERS TO BELIEVE THAT OLD STICK-EATERS TALE ABOUT A DEVIL THAT THE DRAGONS TURNED TO STONE?
. . . YOU'RE SERIOUS!
THE EARTH TREMBLES, MY FRIEND. THE LORD OF THE LOCUSTS MAY SOON WALK AMONG US.
IF THE QUEEN AND HER GRANDDAUGHTER WERE TO FALL INTO THE WRONG HANDS . . .
BUT LUCIUS WOULD NEVER - -
BOOM

BLOODY STARS! THE MOUNTAIN'S BLOWING UP!
HEADMASTER!
WHAT IS HAPPENING?
THERE IS MOVEMENT BELOW THE GATE!
LOOK OUT!
THE RATS ARE CHARGING!
THE ATTACK BEGINS.
GIVE THE COMMAND.
LOOK! LOOK!
THE VILLAGERS - -
MY FAMILY - -
TO YOUR POSTS.
MOVE! MOVE!
THEY'RE COMING!
OVER HERE..
THIS IS IT, TINSMITH. GO TO YOUR PEOPLE AND LEAD THEM WELL.
AAAIEE!
AAAAH!
AAAH!
AAAA--
AAAAAIEEII!!!
CRANG
AAAAAH
CLANG
CRASH

BOOM
BUH BOOM
RRRRRRRUMMMBLE
KTOOM!
SHAASH!
KRAK!
FOOM!

COME ON! GIVE ME YOUR HAND!
BOOM
THIS IS CRAZY! WE'LL NEVER GET OFF THIS MOUNTAIN BEFORE IT EXPLODES!
KEEP MOVING!
KRAAAK
POM
FONE BONE! LOOK OUT!
CHUNK!

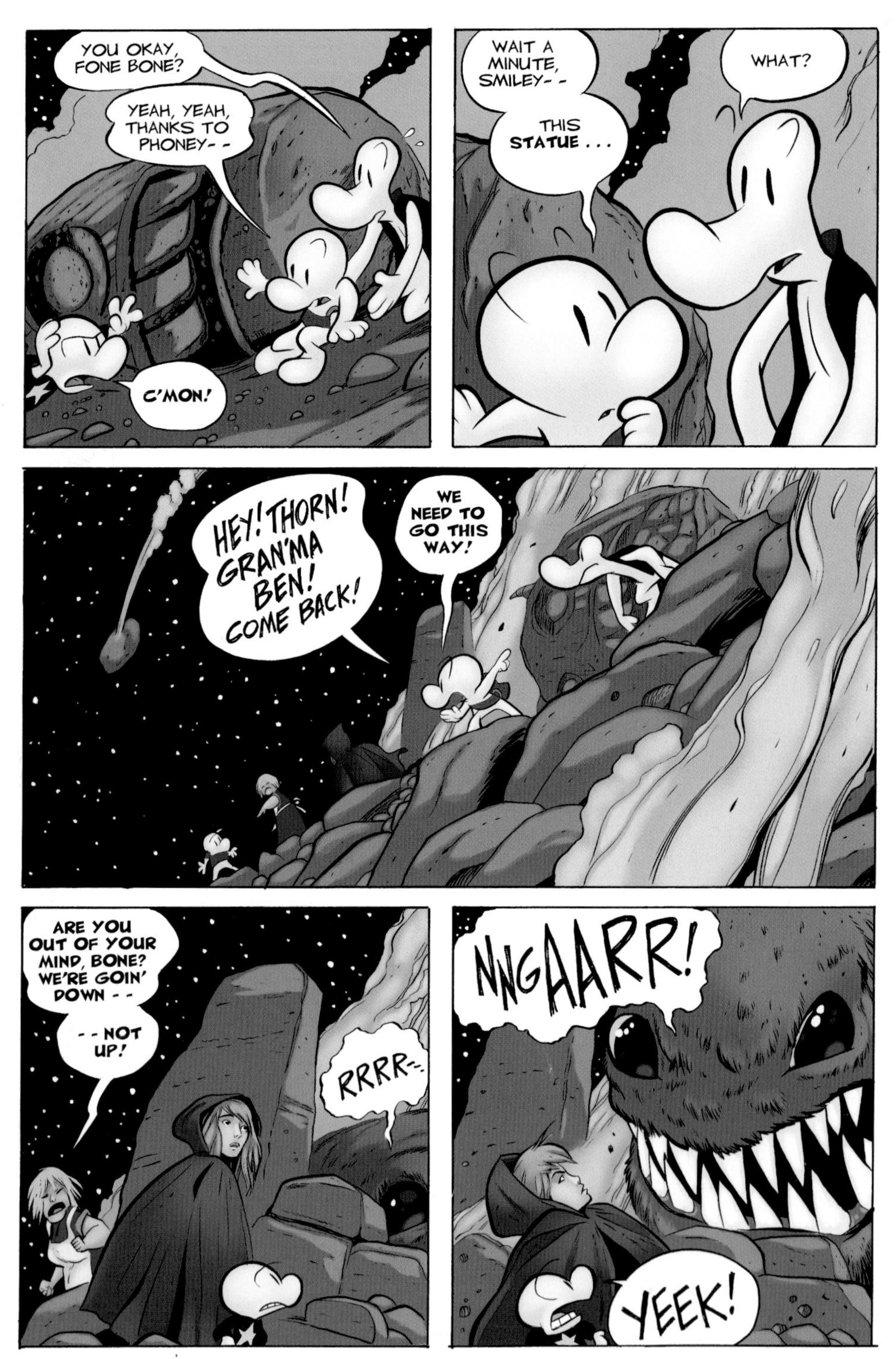
YOU OKAY, FONE BONE?
YEAH, YEAH, THANKS TO PHONEY- -
C'MON!
WAIT A MINUTE, SMILEY- -
THIS STATUE . . .
WHAT?
HEY! THORN! GRAN'MA BEN! COME BACK!
WE NEED TO GO THIS WAY!
ARE YOU OUT OF YOUR MIND, BONE? WE'RE GOIN' DOWN - -
- - NOT UP!
RRRR
NNGAARR!
YEEK!

OHMYGOSH.
IT'S KINGDOK! RUN, YOU GUYS!
RRRRRR...
THORN! RUN!
WHAT ARE YOU DOING?!
RRRRR...
NGAHH!
CRUNCH!

RRRAAGH! KILL YOO!
GO! GO!
TAKE THEM, BONE! QUICK!
HERE HE COMES!!
KUH-- KILL YOOU!
EERF!
OW! OW!
GET UP THERE!
SMASH!

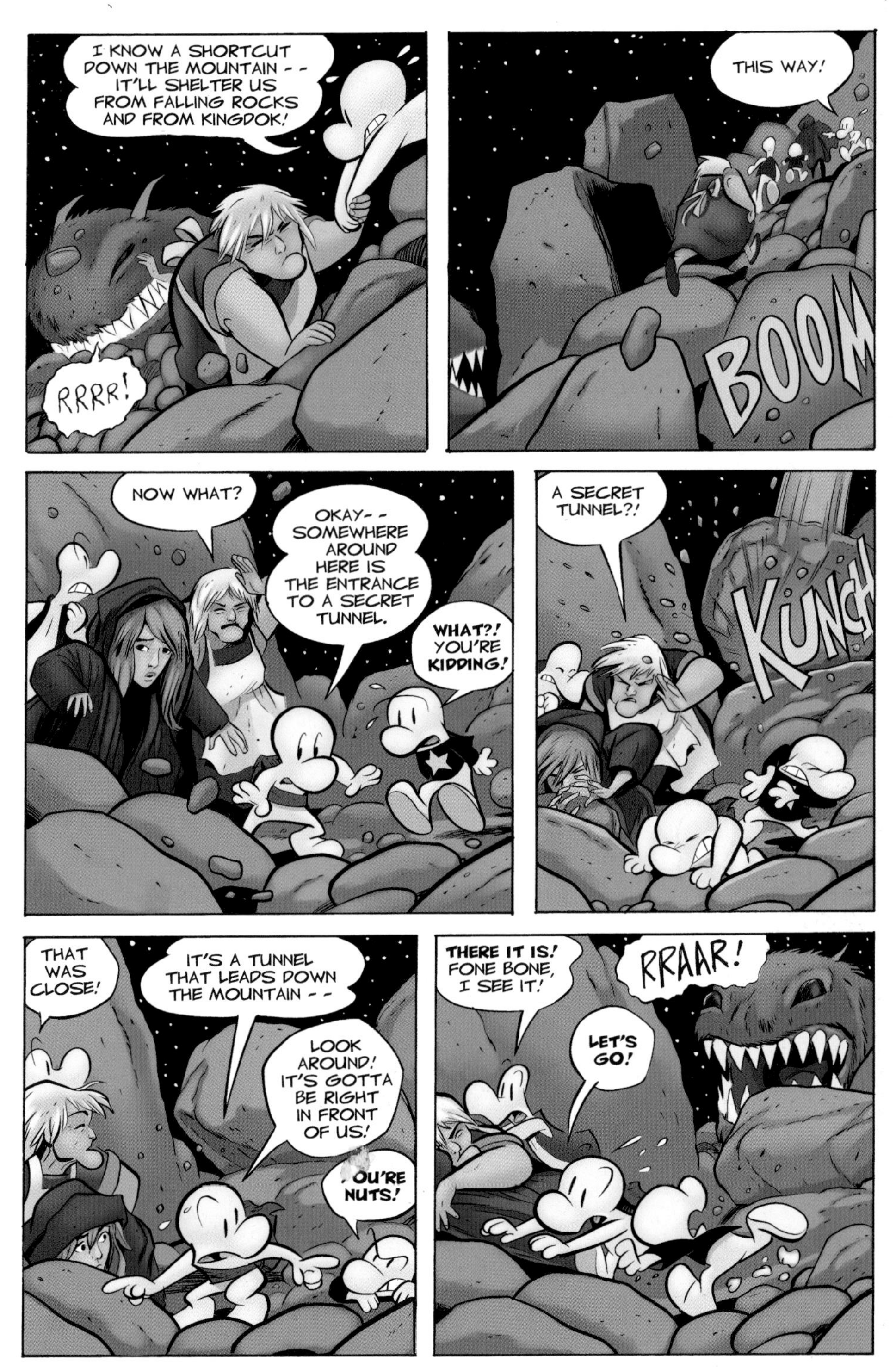
I KNOW A SHORTCUT DOWN THE MOUNTAIN - - IT'LL SHELTER US FROM FALLING ROCKS AND FROM KINGDOK!
RRRR!
THIS WAY!
BOOM
NOW WHAT?
OKAY- - SOMEWHERE AROUND HERE IS THE ENTRANCE TO A SECRET TUNNEL.
WHAT?! YOU'RE KIDDING!
A SECRET TUNNEL?!
KUNCH
THAT WAS CLOSE!
IT'S A TUNNEL THAT LEADS DOWN THE MOUNTAIN - -
LOOK AROUND! IT'S GOTTA BE RIGHT IN FRONT OF US!
OU'RE NUTS!
THERE IT IS! FONE BONE, I SEE IT!
RRAAR!
LET'S GO!

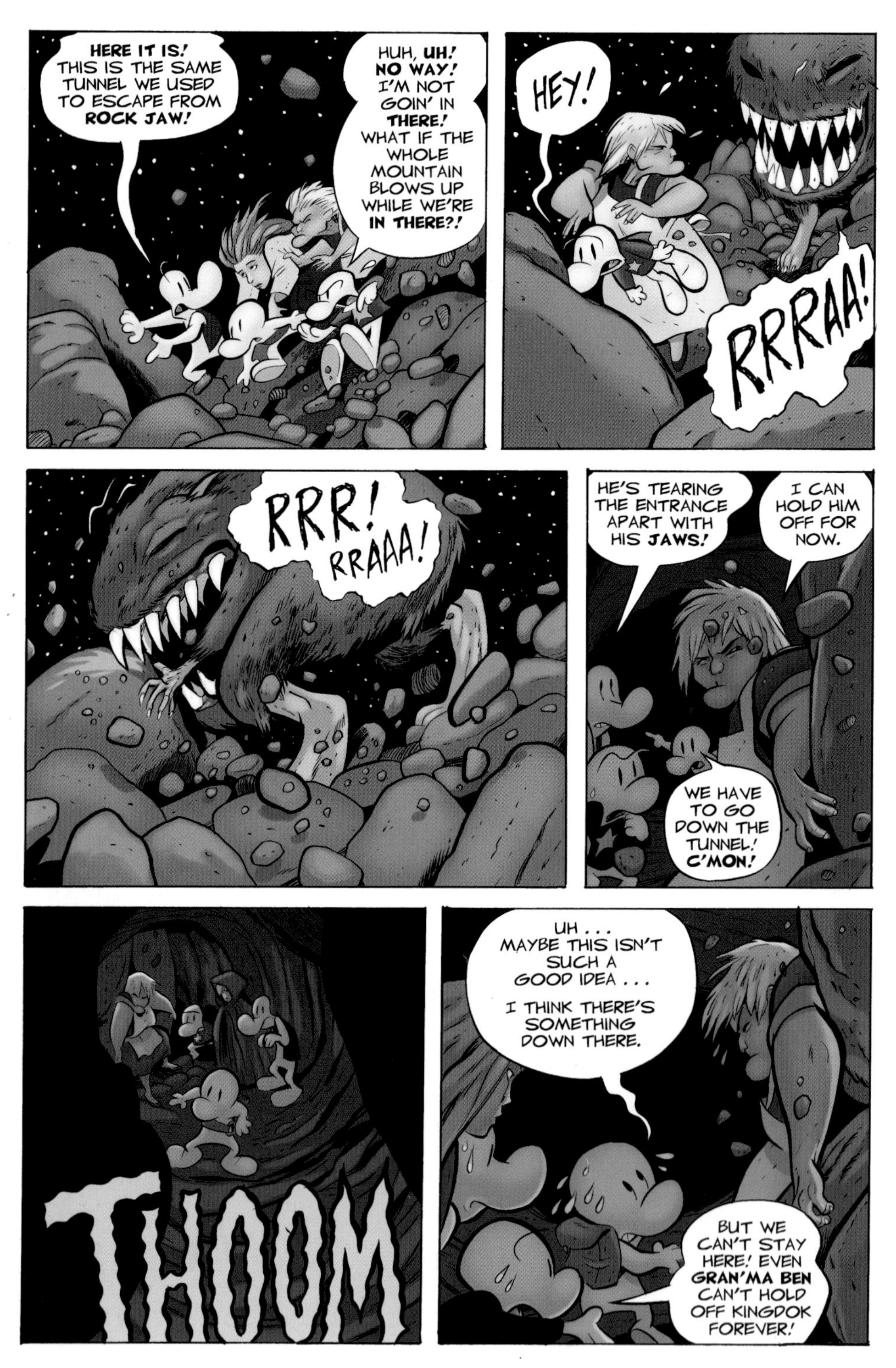
HERE IT IS! THIS IS THE SAME TUNNEL WE USED TO ESCAPE FROM ROCK JAW!
HUH, UH! NO WAY! I'M NOT GOIN' IN THERE! WHAT IF THE WHOLE MOUNTAIN BLOWS UP WHILE WE'RE IN THERE?!
HEY!
RRRAA!
RRR! RRAAA!
HE'S TEARING THE ENTRANCE APART WITH HIS JAWS!
I CAN HOLD HIM OFF FOR NOW.
WE HAVE TO GO DOWN THE TUNNEL! C'MON!
THOOM
UH . . . MAYBE THIS ISN'T SUCH A GOOD IDEA . . .
I THINK THERE'S SOMETHING DOWN THERE.
BUT WE CAN'T STAY HERE! EVEN GRAN'MA BEN CAN'T HOLD OFF KINGDOK FOREVER!

WELL... UH... I GUESS WE HAVE TO GO DOWN THEN.
FONE BONE! WHAT ABOUT THE DREAMS?
WHAT DREAMS?
DON'T YOU REMEMBER? THIS TUNNEL LEADS TO THE OLD RAT CREATURE TEMPLE!
OH, MY GOSH! THAT'S RIGHT! AND WE ALL BEGAN TO HALLUCINATE!
OH, GREAT.
GRAN'MA! SMILEY AND I HAVE BEEN HERE BEFORE. THERE'S A GOOD CHANCE THAT IF WE GO INTO THIS TUNNEL, WE --
WE'LL BE OVERWHELMED BY NIGHTMARES, I KNOW...
I'VE BEEN HERE BEFORE AS WELL. A LONG, LONG TIME AGO.
THOOM
THERE'S THAT NOISE AGAIN!
WHAT THE HECK IS THAT?

FOLLOW ME.
WE WILL BE SAFE IN THE OLD TEMPLE.
WHEN I LET GO, **KINGDOK** IS COMING IN.
YOU READY?
WELL, ACTUALLY, I WAS HAVING SECOND THOU- -
ON YOUR FEET, BOYS!
AAAH!

RRUMMBL
POP!
POW!
RRRUMMMMBLE
RUMMBLE
KRA

HEADMASTER! AN ARMY FROM PAWA IS GATHERING AT THE SOUTHERN ARCH.
GO THERE. TAKE AS MANY OF THE VILLAGERS AS ARE WILLING TO FOLLOW - -
BUH-DOOM
THE MOUNTAIN!

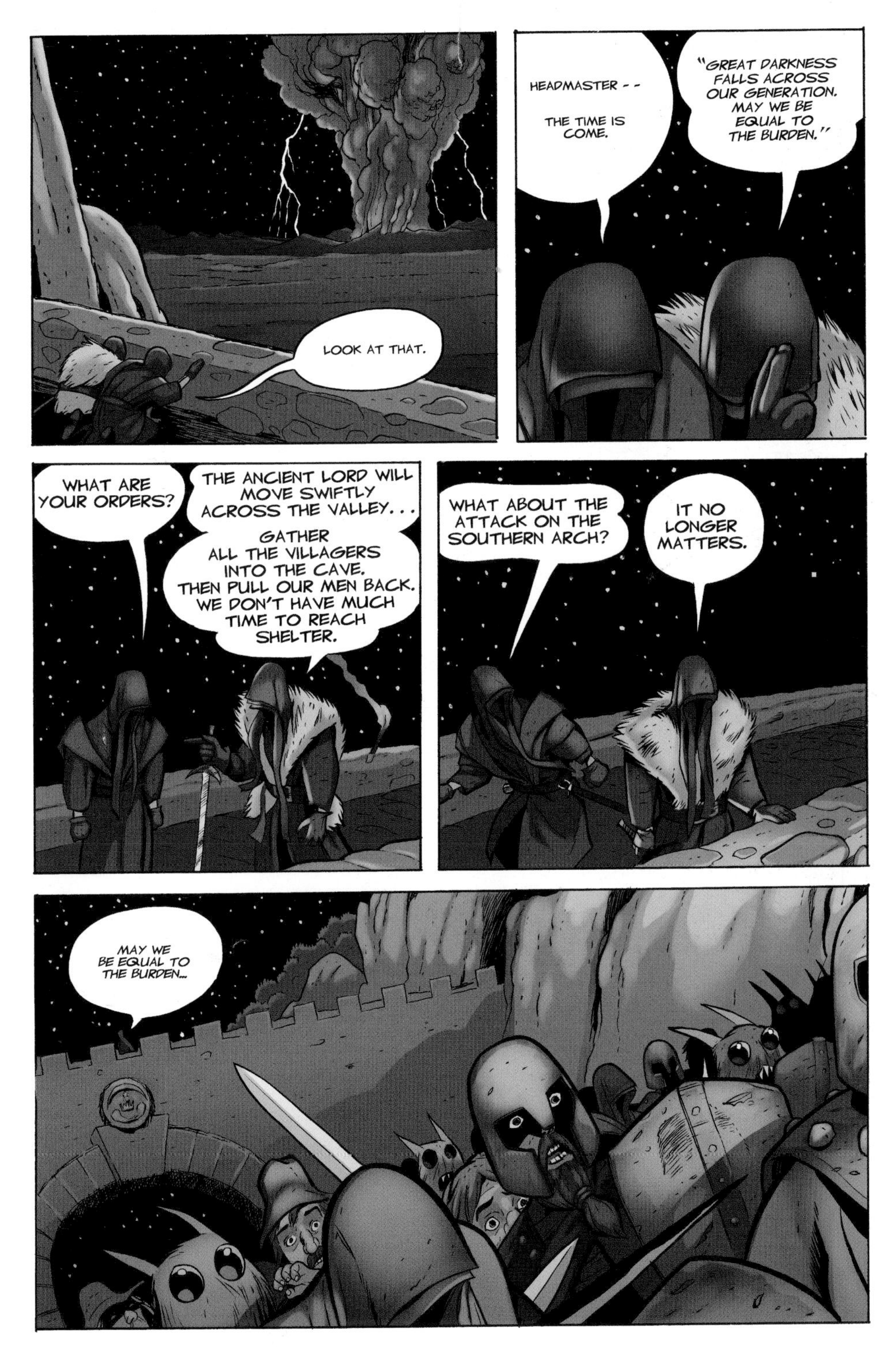
LOOK AT THAT.
HEADMASTER - -
THE TIME IS COME.
"GREAT DARKNESS FALLS ACROSS OUR GENERATION. MAY WE BE EQUAL TO THE BURDEN."
WHAT ARE YOUR ORDERS?
THE ANCIENT LORD WILL MOVE SWIFTLY ACROSS THE VALLEY. . .
GATHER ALL THE VILLAGERS INTO THE CAVE. THEN PULL OUR MEN BACK. WE DON'T HAVE MUCH TIME TO REACH SHELTER.
WHAT ABOUT THE ATTACK ON THE SOUTHERN ARCH?
IT NO LONGER MATTERS.
MAY WE BE EQUAL TO THE BURDEN...

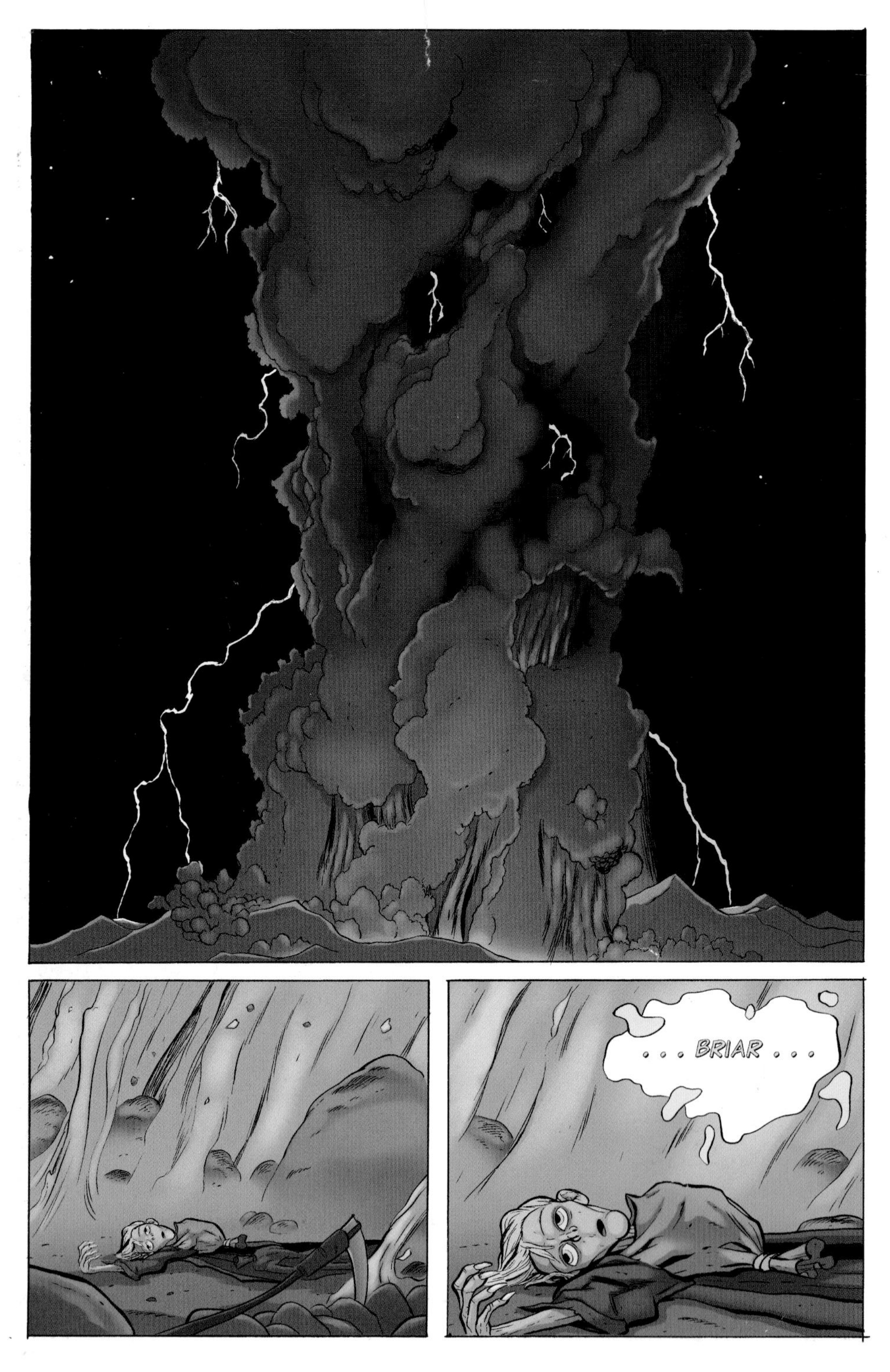
. . . BRIAR . . .

. . . ARISE, BRIAR . . .
GURK--GKK--
GGGRRRKKK---
MASTER . . . ? ARE YOU . . . ? FREE . . . ? DOES THE LORD OF THE LOCUSTS ROAM THE EARTH AT LAST?
NO.

NO. . . ? BUT I GATHERED TOGETHER ALL THE FORCES NECESSARY TO **FREE** YOU - - ?
YOU GATHERED THEM IN THE WRONG CONFIGURATION.
BECAUSE OF YOUR TREASON, ONLY PART OF OUR POWERS ESCAPED. . .
MY LORD . . . I BEG YOUR FORGIVENESS . . . . I - - WAS BLINDED BY MY JEALOUSY OF THE YOUNG PRINCESS - -
YOU MUST SEEK OUT OUR MISSING POWERS AND RETURN THEM TO US . . .
I WILL FIND THEM AT ONCE, MY LORD.
QUICKLY, MY PETS . . . COME TO ME . . .
YESSS . . . YESS . . . GOOD . . .

COME, COME...
LET US GET UP...
MMMM...
HEEE HEE
WELL, MY PETS...
IT LOOKS AS IF WE ARE NEEDED AFTER ALL.

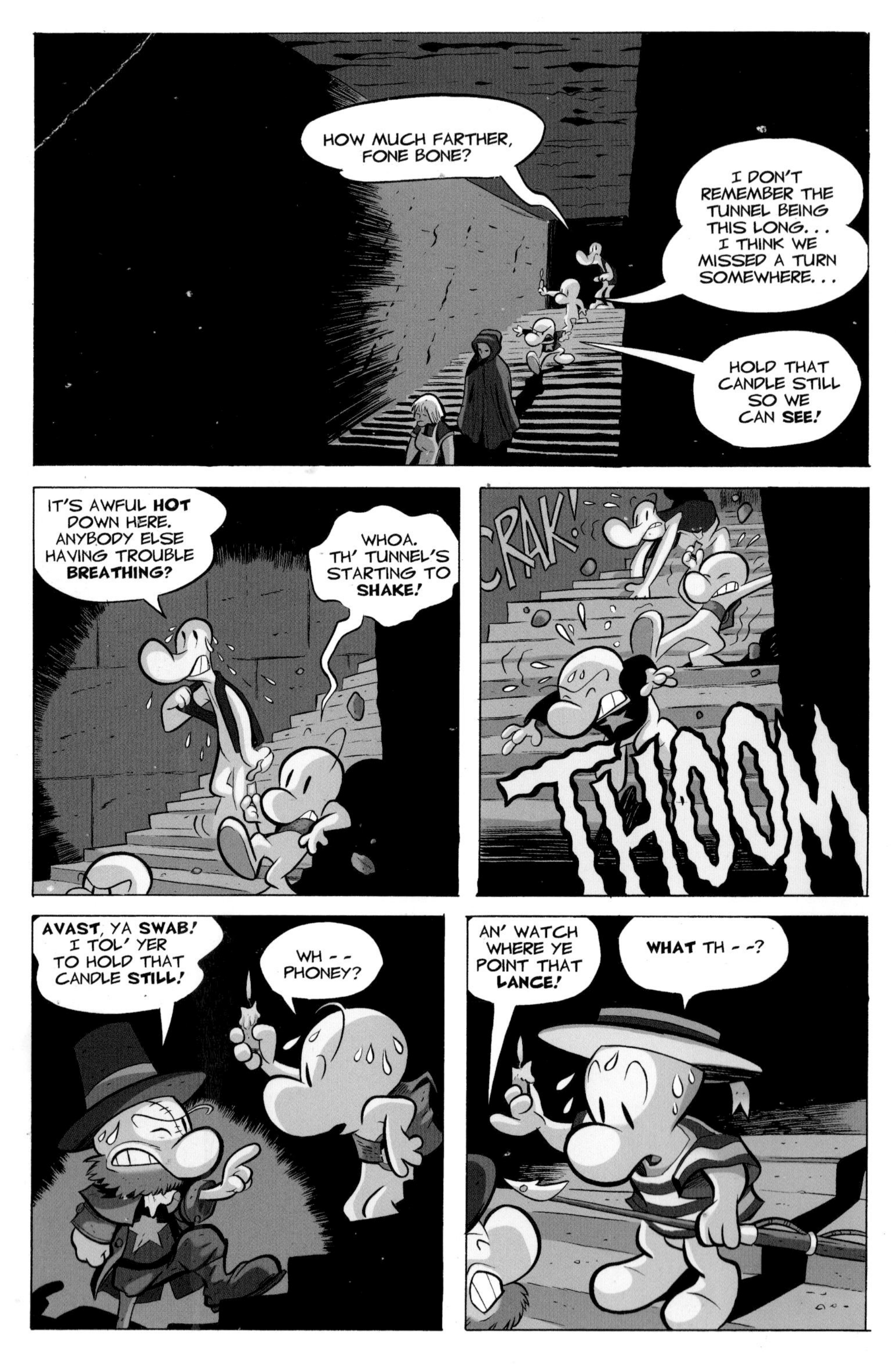
HOW MUCH FARTHER, FONE BONE?
I DON'T REMEMBER THE TUNNEL BEING THIS LONG. . . I THINK WE MISSED A TURN SOMEWHERE. . .
HOLD THAT CANDLE STILL SO WE CAN SEE!
IT'S AWFUL HOT DOWN HERE. ANYBODY ELSE HAVING TROUBLE BREATHING?
WHOA. TH' TUNNEL'S STARTING TO SHAKE!
CRAK!
THOOM
AVAST, YA SWAB! I TOL' YER TO HOLD THAT CANDLE STILL!
WH - - PHONEY?
AN' WATCH WHERE YE POINT THAT LANCE!
WHAT TH - -?

SOMETHIN' WRONG, FONE BONE?
UM. I'M NOT SURE . . . BUT I HAVE A HARPOON.
ARRR! WHAT'D I TELL YER ABOUT THAT CANDLE, ISHMAEL?
ISN'T THAT CUTE? PHONEY'S GOT A LITTLE HAT ON!
I DO? HEY! WHERE'S MY LEG?!
EVERYBODY STAY CALM. THIS IS JUST A HALLUCINATION! WE'RE PROBABLY BREATHING SOME UNDERGROUND GAS OR SOMETHING.
NO, WE'RE NOT! IT'S THE POWER OF THE DREAMING!
BUT I ONLY HAVE ONE LEG!
YOU ONLY HAVE ONE EYE, TOO!
SMILEY, THE DREAMING IS JUST A LOCAL SUPERSTITION - -
AAAH!
PHONEY! IT'S NOT REAL! GET A HOLD OF YOURSELF!
IT'S A DREAM CAUSED BY THE MYSTICAL POWERS OF THE EARTH ITSELF - -
OH, COME ON! A MASS HALLUCINATION LIKE THIS MUST BE CAUSED BY A SUBSTANCE THAT HAS A CHEMICAL EFFECT ON OUR BRAINS, NOT BY MYSTICAL POWERS!
OH, YEAH? LIKE WHAT?

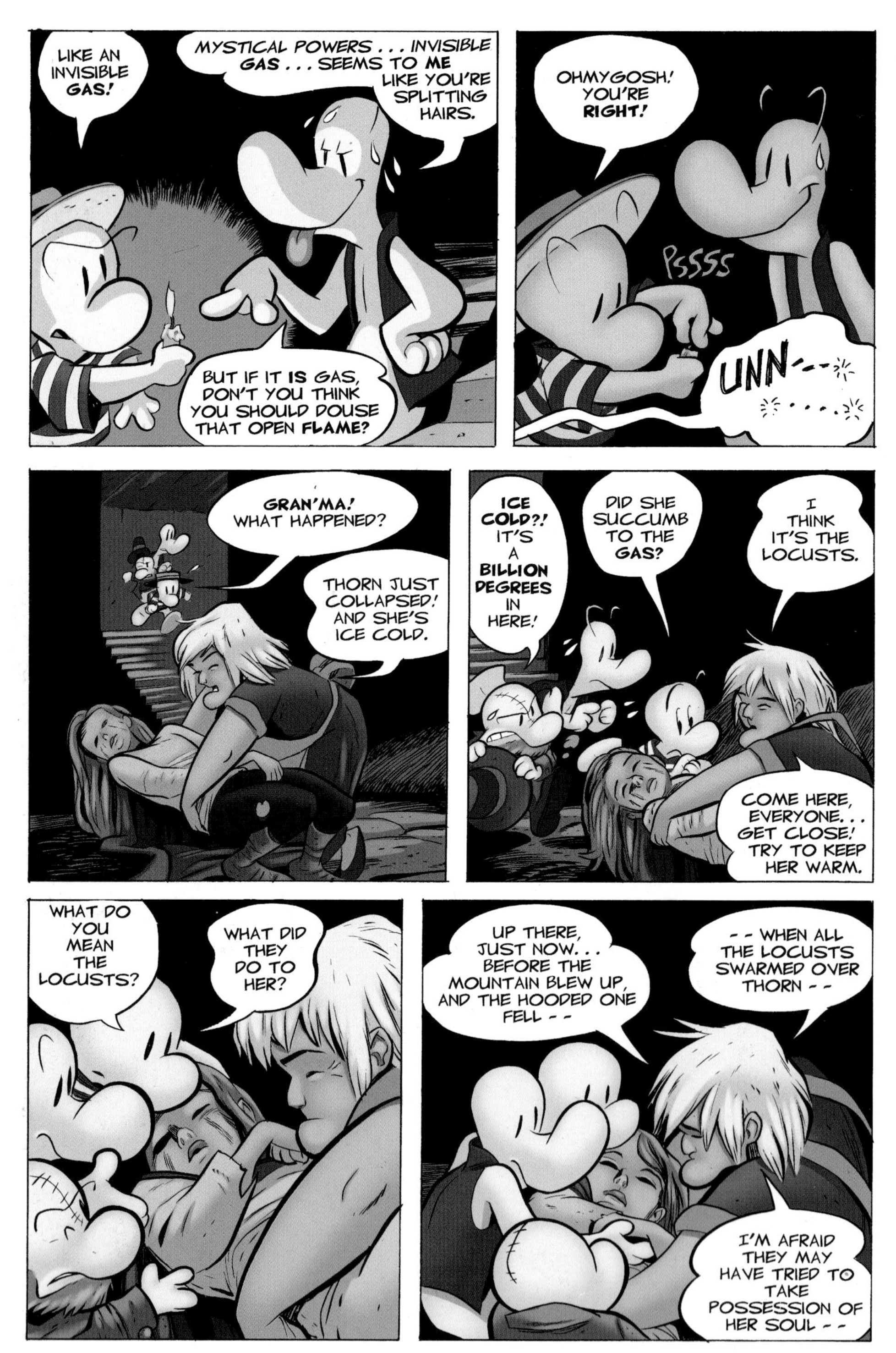
LIKE AN INVISIBLE GAS!
MYSTICAL POWERS . . . INVISIBLE GAS . . . SEEMS TO ME LIKE YOU'RE SPLITTING HAIRS.
BUT IF IT IS GAS, DON'T YOU THINK YOU SHOULD DOUSE THAT OPEN FLAME?
OHMYGOSH! YOU'RE RIGHT!
PSSSS
UNN- - - . . . .
GRAN'MA! WHAT HAPPENED?
THORN JUST COLLAPSED! AND SHE'S ICE COLD.
ICE COLD?! IT'S A BILLION DEGREES IN HERE!
DID SHE SUCCUMB TO THE GAS?
I THINK IT'S THE LOCUSTS.
COME HERE, EVERYONE. . . GET CLOSE! TRY TO KEEP HER WARM.
WHAT DO YOU MEAN THE LOCUSTS?
WHAT DID THEY DO TO HER?
UP THERE, JUST NOW. . . BEFORE THE MOUNTAIN BLEW UP, AND THE HOODED ONE FELL - -
- - WHEN ALL THE LOCUSTS SWARMED OVER THORN - -
I'M AFRAID THEY MAY HAVE TRIED TO TAKE POSSESSION OF HER SOUL - -

SHE'S WAKING UP!
WHERE AM I?
SHHH. YOU'RE WITH US, DEAR. YOU'RE SAFE.
I SPOKE WITH THE LORD OF THE LOCUSTS.
YES. I KNOW.
SO DID I. RIGHT HERE IN THIS VERY CAVE, A LONG, LONG TIME AGO.
TELL ME ABOUT THAT.
WELL, DEAR, ONE DAY WHEN I WAS YOUR AGE, I FOLLOWED MY OLDER SISTER BRIAR HERE. THE LORD OF THE LOCUSTS WAS WAITING FOR US.
I'M AFRAID IT WASN'T VERY PLEASANT.
OUR BODIES WERE COVERED WITH LOCUSTS . . . JUST LIKE YOURS WAS. HE WAS SEARCHING FOR SOMETHING . . .
YOUR DREAMING EYE.
YES, THAT'S RIGHT. HE WAS SEARCHING FOR MY DREAMING EYE. TELL ME, THORN. DID THE LORD OF THE LOCUSTS FIND **YOUR** DREAMING EYE?
ALMOST.
FONE BONE STOPPED HIM.
LET ME UP. WE NEED TO GET MOVING.

THORN, ARE YOU SURE YOU'RE OKAY?
YES. BUT I'M WORRIED ABOUT THE VALLEY. WE NEED TO GET OUT OF THIS CAVE.
THERE'S LIGHT COMING FROM UP AHEAD. . .
SO TELL ME, GRAN'MA, WHO ELSE HAS A DREAMING EYE BESIDES YOU AND ME?
WHY, EVERYONE HAS ONE, DEAR . . .
SOME ARE MORE OPEN THAN OTHERS, BUT IT'S THE PLACE WHERE THE DREAMING FLOWS THROUGH YOU.
SO YOU KNEW HOW POWERFUL BRIAR'S EYE WAS.
WELL, NO. BRIAR'S EYE WAS BLIND FROM BIRTH, AND I THINK SHE HAD TROUBLES BECAUSE OF IT. SHE COULDN'T TELL RIGHT FROM WRONG.
HMM. WHO TOLD YOU BRIAR'S DREAMING EYE WAS BLIND?
BRIAR DID.
IT WASN'T TRUE?
NO. AND NOT ONLY WAS BRIAR'S DREAMING EYE NEVER BLIND, IF I'M NOT MISTAKEN, IT'S STILL OPEN!
HEY! THE GATE'S THIS WAY!

OW! IT'S SO BRIGHT! MY EYES AREN'T USED TO IT!
WHO CARES! AT LEAST WE'RE OUTTA THAT HOLE!
HEY - - IS IT SNOWING?
NO. IT'S ASH! LOOK! THERE'S ASH ALL OVER THE GROUND. WHAT'S GOING ON?
OH, NO . . .
LOOK!
IT'S GONE . . .
WHAT'S GONE?
EVERYTHING. THE WHOLE VALLEY . . .
IT'S ALL GONE.

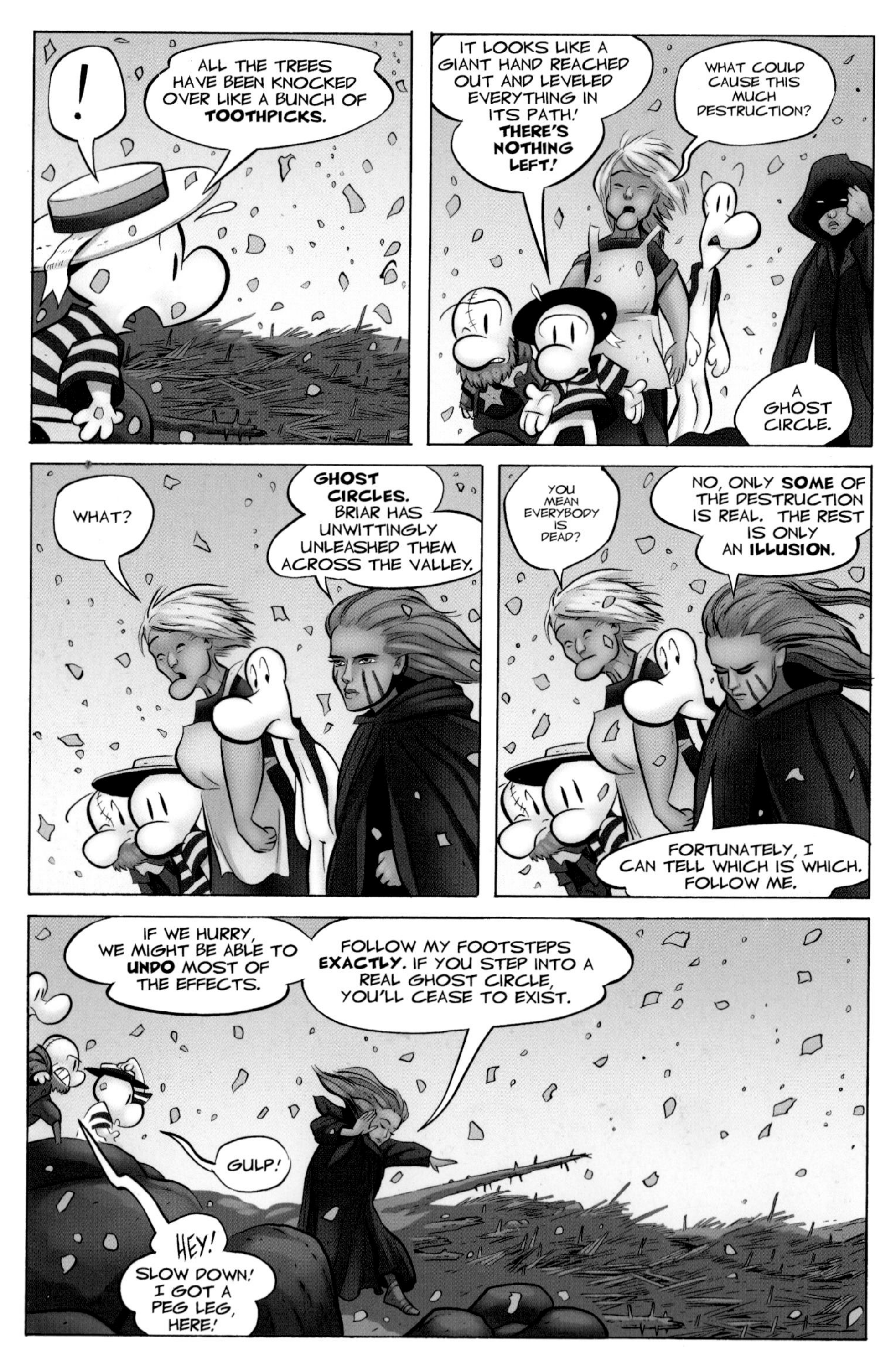
!
ALL THE TREES HAVE BEEN KNOCKED OVER LIKE A BUNCH OF TOOTHPICKS.
IT LOOKS LIKE A GIANT HAND REACHED OUT AND LEVELED EVERYTHING IN ITS PATH! THERE'S NOTHING LEFT!
WHAT COULD CAUSE THIS MUCH DESTRUCTION?
A GHOST CIRCLE.
WHAT?
GHOST CIRCLES. BRIAR HAS UNWITTINGLY UNLEASHED THEM ACROSS THE VALLEY.
YOU MEAN EVERYBODY IS DEAD?
NO, ONLY SOME OF THE DESTRUCTION IS REAL. THE REST IS ONLY AN ILLUSION.
FORTUNATELY, I CAN TELL WHICH IS WHICH. FOLLOW ME.
IF WE HURRY, WE MIGHT BE ABLE TO UNDO MOST OF THE EFFECTS.
FOLLOW MY FOOTSTEPS EXACTLY. IF YOU STEP INTO A REAL GHOST CIRCLE, YOU'LL CEASE TO EXIST.
GULP!
HEY! SLOW DOWN! I GOT A PEG LEG, HERE!

THORN. WAIT! DO YOU REALLY THINK YOU CAN UNDO ALL THIS? HOW?
I DON'T KNOW YET, BUT REMEMBER WHEN THE LORD OF THE LOCUSTS TRIED TO POSSESS MY BODY . . . AND YOU PUT THIS DRAGON-NECKLACE ON ME, FORCING HIM TO FLEE?
WELL, BEFORE HE LEFT, I MANAGED TO TEAR A LITTLE PIECE OFF HIM AND KEEP IT.
SO NOW I HAVE SOME OF HIS POWERS, I GUESS.
REMEMBER TO WATCH WHERE I STEP! WE DON'T HAVE MUCH TIME.
ARRH!

BONE
HEY! FONE BONE!
ISN'T THERE AN EASIER WAY TO GO BESIDES CLIMBING OVER EVERY TREE IN OUR PATH?!
FOR THE MILLIONTH TIME, NO!
WE HAVE TO FOLLOW THORN'S FOOTSTEPS EXACTLY.
NOW STOP FUSSING ABOUT, PHONEY. THIS IS DANGEROUS! ALL THIS ASH IS SLIPPERY!
IT'S HARD ENOUGH TO SEE AND BREATHE . . .
. . . BUT IF YOU MAKE SMILEY SLIDE OFF THE PATH INTO A GHOST CIRCLE - -
YOU'LL BOTH DIE.
YEAH, YEAH, RIGHT. GHOST CIRCLES. WHAT THE HECK ARE THEY ANYWAY?

TRY TO IMAGINE THAT WE'RE SURROUNDED BY GIANT INVISIBLE BUBBLES. . .
. . . BUBBLES FILLED WITH SUPERNATURAL EVIL!
THERE'S NOT ENOUGH DESTRUCTION AROUND, WE GOTTA HAVE EVIL, TOO?
IT'S A VOLCANO! CAN'T WE JUST SAY THE MOUNTAIN BLEW UP? WHY'S IT EVIL?
LOOK, I DON'T UNDERSTAND WHAT'S GOING ON ANY BETTER THAN YOU DO . . .
BUT IF THORN AND GRAN'MA BEN SAY WE TIPTOE AROUND THESE GHOST AREAS, THEN WE TIPTOE!
FINE.
FINE!
BUT IF YOU ASK ME - -
I'M NOT ASKIN' YOU.
FINE! BUT IF YOU ASK ME, I'D SAY YOU'RE LETTIN' THOSE TWO WOMEN GET TO YOU WITH THEIR TALK ABOUT DREAMS AND DRAGONS AND EVIL SPIRITS!
IT'S ALL A BUNCH OF HOOEY!

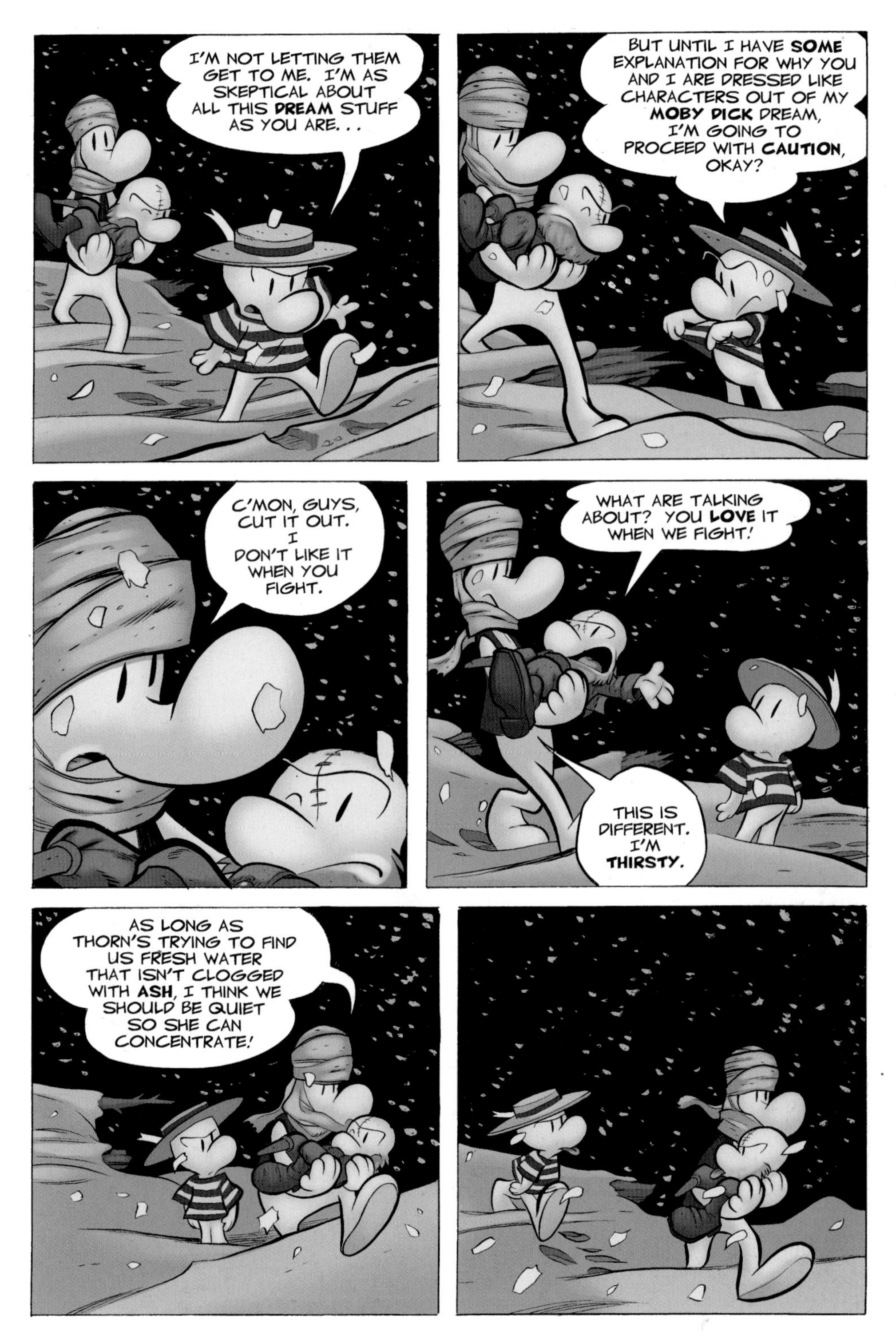
I'M NOT LETTING THEM GET TO ME. I'M AS SKEPTICAL ABOUT ALL THIS DREAM STUFF AS YOU ARE. . .
BUT UNTIL I HAVE SOME EXPLANATION FOR WHY YOU AND I ARE DRESSED LIKE CHARACTERS OUT OF MY MOBY DICK DREAM, I'M GOING TO PROCEED WITH CAUTION, OKAY?
C'MON, GUYS, CUT IT OUT. I DON'T LIKE IT WHEN YOU FIGHT.
WHAT ARE TALKING ABOUT? YOU LOVE IT WHEN WE FIGHT!
THIS IS DIFFERENT. I'M THIRSTY.
AS LONG AS THORN'S TRYING TO FIND US FRESH WATER THAT ISN'T CLOGGED WITH ASH, I THINK WE SHOULD BE QUIET SO SHE CAN CONCENTRATE!

WAIT. . .

THE WAY AHEAD IS NARROW- - WATCH MY FOOTSTEPS CAREFULLY- -
AND THAT ROCK IS OFF-LIMITS.
JEEZ! BE CAREFUL YOU LUNKHEAD, MY PEG LEG ALMOST TOUCHED THE ROCK.
RRR.
WE NEED TO STOP. I'M GETTING TIRED.
HOW CAN YOU BE TIRED?!! YOU'RE BEING CARRIED!
DO YOU EVER THINK ABOUT ANYTHING OTHER THAN YOURSELF?!
WHAT ABOUT THE REST OF US WHO ARE JUST TRYING TO SURVIVE THE MESS YOU MADE?!
WHA- -
WAIT- -
WHAT?
ARE YOU SAYIN' THIS IS MY FAULT?

PUT ME DOWN.
LET ME JUST WADDLE OVER HERE - -
ON MY LEG MADE OF WHALE BONE - -
AND POINT OUT THAT I'M NOT THE ONE WHO'S OBSESSED WITH MOBY DICK!
YOU DID THIS TO ME, REMEMBER?
I'M NOT OBSESSED, AND DON'T CHANGE THE SUBJECT! YOU'RE THE ONE WHO GOT US RUN OUT OF BONEVILLE WITH THAT STUPID CAMPAIGN BALLOON!
CHANGE THE SUBJECT?! LOOK AT ME! I'M CAPTAIN AHAB!
MM. WELL, MAYBE THAT IS MY FAULT. . .
I CAN'T REALLY FIGURE THAT OUT.
WELL, I CAN! EVERYBODY IN THIS VALLEY IS NUTS! INCLUDING US!
WE NEED TO GET OUTTA HERE BEFORE IT'S TOO LATE! AND YOU'RE THE ONLY ONE WHO'S STOPPING US!
WHAT?!
I'M THE ONE WHO WANTS TO GO HOME!
NO, YOU'RE NOT! I KEEP COMING UP WITH ESCAPE PLANS, BUT YOU DON'T WANT TO GO! YOU WANNA STAY HERE AND HELP PEOPLE! REMEMBER RUNNING OUT ON ME SO YOU COULD HELP A BABY RAT CREATURE OR WHATEVER?

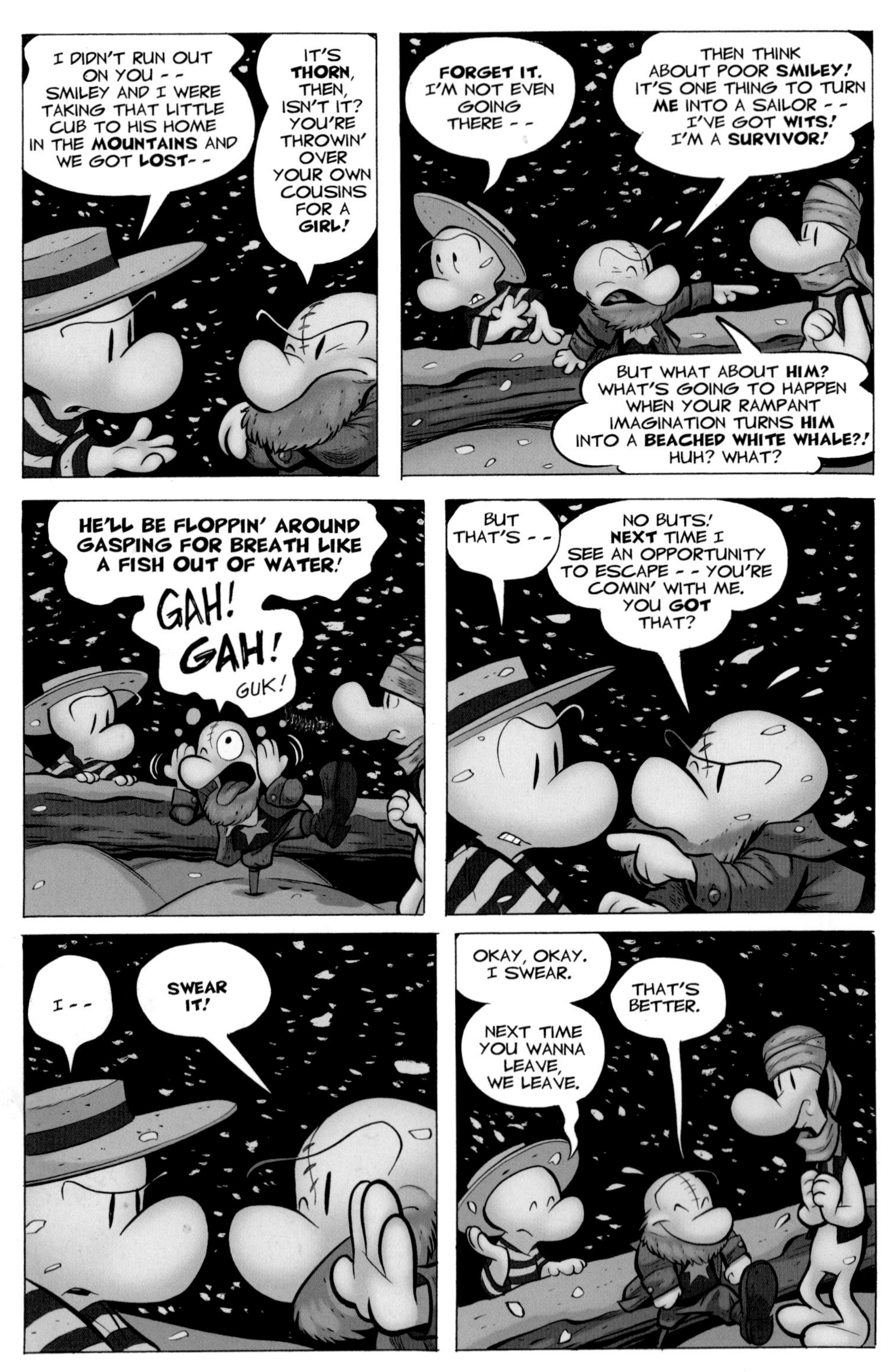
I DIDN'T RUN OUT ON YOU - - SMILEY AND I WERE TAKING THAT LITTLE CUB TO HIS HOME IN THE MOUNTAINS AND WE GOT LOST- -
IT'S THORN, THEN, ISN'T IT? YOU'RE THROWIN' OVER YOUR OWN COUSINS FOR A GIRL!
FORGET IT. I'M NOT EVEN GOING THERE - -
THEN THINK ABOUT POOR SMILEY! IT'S ONE THING TO TURN ME INTO A SAILOR - - I'VE GOT WITS! I'M A SURVIVOR!
BUT WHAT ABOUT HIM? WHAT'S GOING TO HAPPEN WHEN YOUR RAMPANT IMAGINATION TURNS HIM INTO A BEACHED WHITE WHALE?! HUH? WHAT?
HE'LL BE FLOPPIN' AROUND GASPING FOR BREATH LIKE A FISH OUT OF WATER!
GAH! GAH!
GUK!
BUT THAT'S - -
NO BUTS! NEXT TIME I SEE AN OPPORTUNITY TO ESCAPE - - YOU'RE COMIN' WITH ME. YOU GOT THAT?
I - -
SWEAR IT!
OKAY, OKAY. I SWEAR.
NEXT TIME YOU WANNA LEAVE, WE LEAVE.
THAT'S BETTER.

BESIDES - - IF THERE'S ANYONE TO BLAME, IT'S THAT CRAZY OL' BAT GRAN'MA BEN! SHE'S BEEN KEEPIN' SECRETS FOR YEARS!
SHE'S KEPT US ALL IN THE DARK!
THE HOODED ONE WAS EVEN HER OWN SISTER AND SHE DIDN'T TELL ANYONE!
GRAN'MA!
GRAN'MA!
ARE YOU ALL RIGHT? WHAT HAPPENED?
THIS. . .
. . . IS WHERE I LEFT LUCIUS.

HE WAS WOUNDED AND COULDN'T WALK . . .
AND NOW HE'S GONE.
JUST LIKE EVERYTHING ELSE . . .
HE'S GONE.
ARE YOU SURE THIS IS WHERE YOU LEFT HIM?
. . . BECAUSE EVERYTHING BEYOND THOSE ROCKS IS AN ILLUSION.
WHAT?
oh, NO...
NO... IT CAN'T BE!
GRAN'MA- -
TAKE IT EASY- -
I LEFT HIM RIGHT HERE--- RIGHT HERE!
GRAM- - shh! shh! LISTEN TO ME - -
IF LUCIUS IS INSIDE A GHOST CIRCLE IT COULD BE THE BEST THING - -

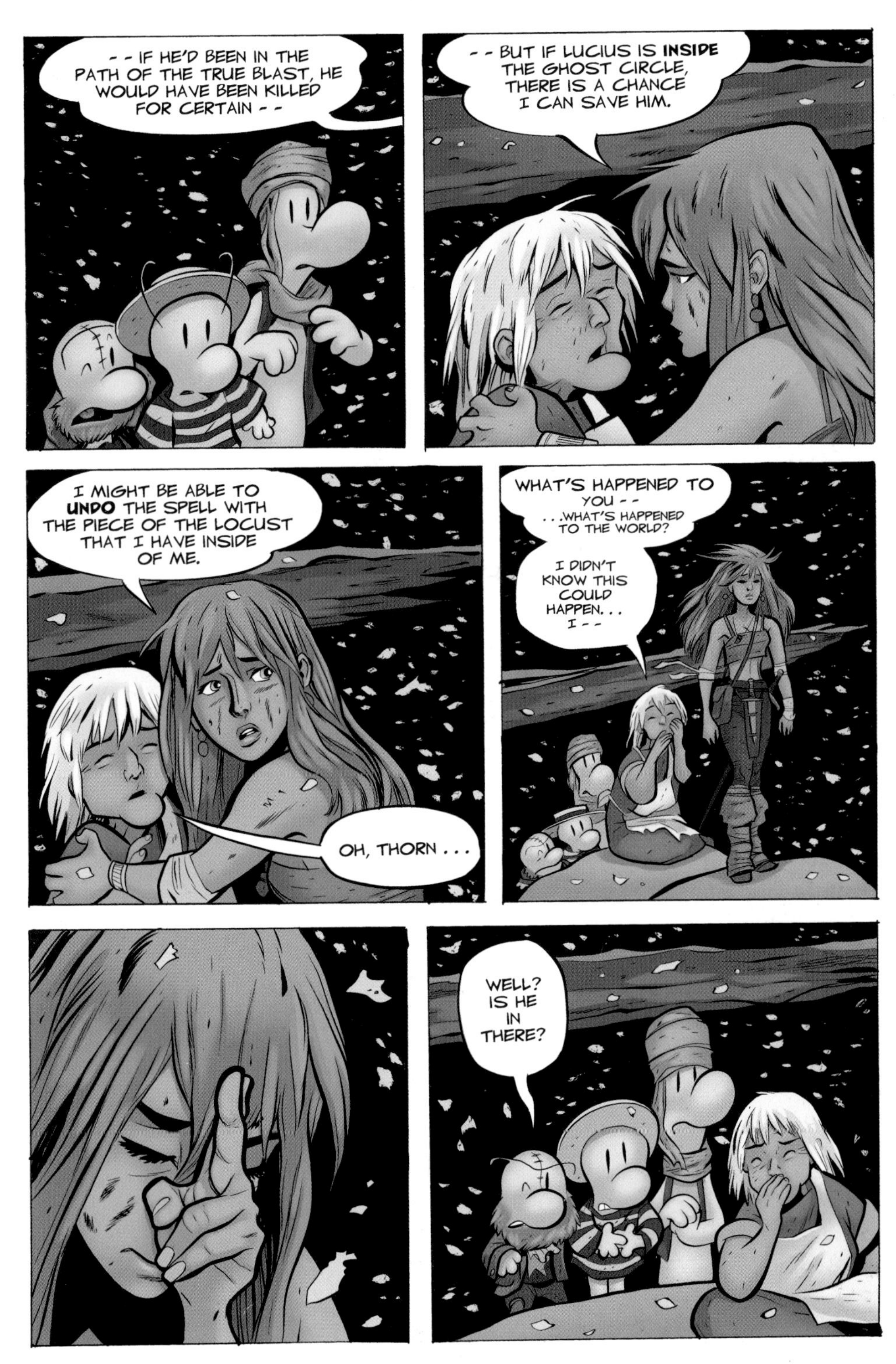
- - IF HE'D BEEN IN THE PATH OF THE TRUE BLAST, HE WOULD HAVE BEEN KILLED FOR CERTAIN - -
- - BUT IF LUCIUS IS INSIDE THE GHOST CIRCLE, THERE IS A CHANCE I CAN SAVE HIM.
I MIGHT BE ABLE TO UNDO THE SPELL WITH THE PIECE OF THE LOCUST THAT I HAVE INSIDE OF ME.
OH, THORN . . .
WHAT'S HAPPENED TO YOU - -
. . .WHAT'S HAPPENED TO THE WORLD?
I DIDN'T KNOW THIS COULD HAPPEN. . . I - -
WELL? IS HE IN THERE?

I CAN'T SEE ANYTHING IN THERE. IT'S ALL SO . . .
. . . SO **CLOUDY** AND **HOT** - -

OKAY - - THAT'S ENOUGH - -
AH! AH! uuh...

OHMYGOSH.

GASP!

AAh!
DID YOU SEE THAT? THERE WERE TREES ALL AROUND US FOR A SECOND.
ho! ho! WHOA!
THAT FELT REALLY WEIRD.
YOU GUYS OKAY?
DID YOU SEE THAT? THERE WERE TREES HERE! EVERYWHERE!
CAREFUL.
DON'T LET GO.
WE'RE JUST INSIDE THE GHOST CIRCLE, BUT I THINK YOU'RE SAFE AS LONG AS YOU HOLD ON TO ME . . .
LET'S BACK UP SLOWLY.
WHAT TREES? WE DIDN'T SEE ANYTHING!
DID YOU SEE LUCIUS?
NO, BUT THE GHOST CIRCLE COVERS A DENSE PART OF THE FOREST. MAYBE WE JUST COULDN'T SEE HIM.
OH, THANK GOODNESS! THE PLACE I LEFT HIM HAD NO TREES!
LUCIUS ISN'T HERE - - WE'RE IN THE WRONG SPOT!

OH, MY, WHAT A RELIEF!
WHAT ABOUT YOU, THORN? ARE YOU ALL RIGHT?
YES, GRAN'MA. I'M JUST A LITTLE TIRED.
I KNOW.
I'M SO SORRY.
WAIT! I HAVE MORE GOOD NEWS! THE SPRING IS OUTSIDE THE GHOST CIRCLE! IT'S JUST OVER THE RIDGE.
SWEET, H2O!
FINALLY! AFTER WE DRINK, CAN WE STOP FOR A WHILE? I'M EXHAUSTED!
YES, PHONCIBLE, WE CAN STOP FOR A REST.
ALL RIGHT, EVERYONE, JUST A LITTLE FARTHER.

WHAT TIME DO YOU THINK IT IS, FONE BONE?
MM? I DON'T KNOW. WITH THE ASH PLUME BLOCKING THE SUN, IT'S HARD TO TELL.
NO, I MEAN WHAT TIME DO YOU THINK IT IS BACK IN BONEVILLE?
WHAT? OH, GEE, I DON'T HAVE ANY IDEA. WHY DO YOU ASK?
I GUESS I'M A LITTLE HOMESICK.
BUT YOU'RE NOT, ARE YOU?
WHAT DO YOU MEAN?

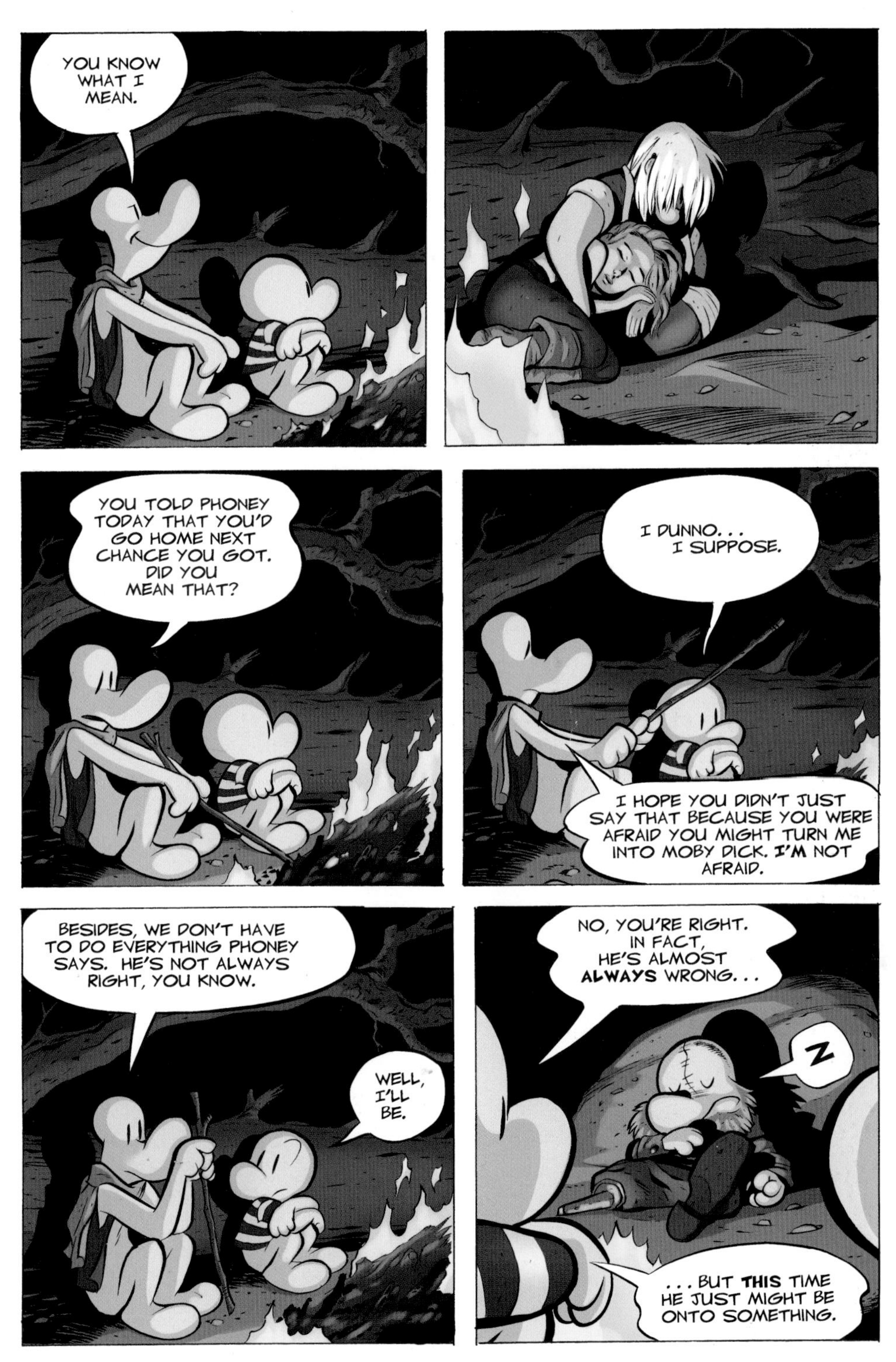
YOU KNOW WHAT I MEAN.
YOU TOLD PHONEY TODAY THAT YOU'D GO HOME NEXT CHANCE YOU GOT. DID YOU MEAN THAT?
I DUNNO. . . I SUPPOSE.
I HOPE YOU DIDN'T JUST SAY THAT BECAUSE YOU WERE AFRAID YOU MIGHT TURN ME INTO MOBY DICK. I'M NOT AFRAID.
BESIDES, WE DON'T HAVE TO DO EVERYTHING PHONEY SAYS. HE'S NOT ALWAYS RIGHT, YOU KNOW.
WELL, I'LL BE.
NO, YOU'RE RIGHT. IN FACT, HE'S ALMOST ALWAYS WRONG. . .
Z
. . . BUT THIS TIME HE JUST MIGHT BE ONTO SOMETHING.

WE DON'T BELONG HERE. . . I MEAN, LOOK AT THESE PEOPLE. THEY BELIEVE IN DREAMS.
I'M AFRAID PHONEY'S RIGHT, ALL THIS DREAMING STUFF IS HOOEY.
YOU DIDN'T THINK IT WAS HOOEY WHEN WE WERE UP ON THE RIDGE AND WE THOUGHT THORN HAD BEEN KILLED.
WHAT ARE YOU TALKING ABOUT?
WE DIDN'T KNOW WHERE THORN WAS. . .
YOU CLOSED YOUR EYES AND YOU COULD TELL - - WITHOUT EVEN SEEING HER - - THAT SHE WAS ALIVE!
WHAT? I DON'T REMEMBER THAT!
I SAW YOU DO IT. I KID YOU NOT.
THAT'S RIDICULOUS!
C'MON, LET'S GET SOME SLEEP BEFORE WE ALL GO COMPLETELY AROUND THE BEND!

PLUP
PLOOP
PISH
MM?
WHA - - ? WHERE AM I?
AAH!

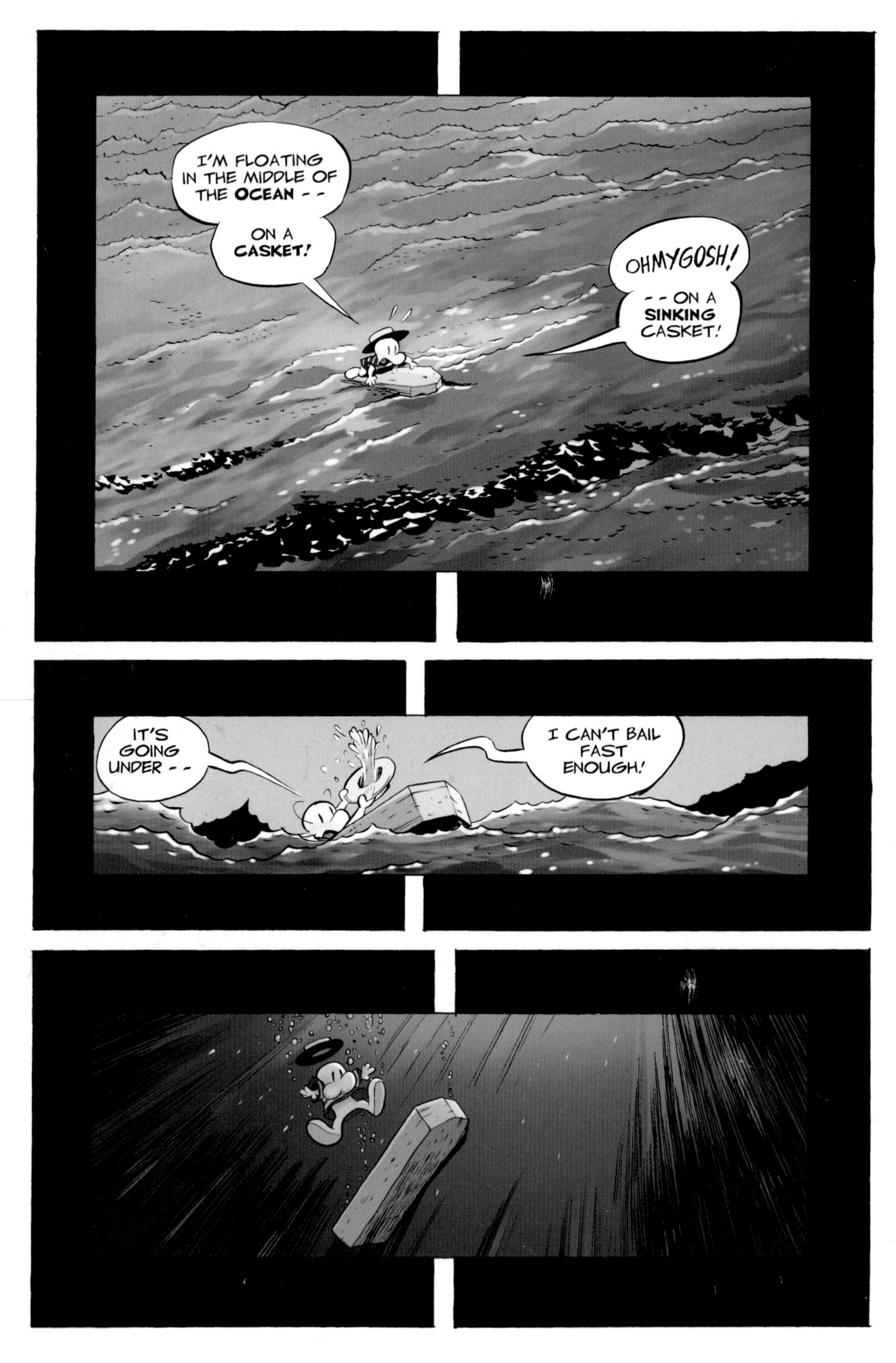
I'M FLOATING IN THE MIDDLE OF THE OCEAN - -
ON A CASKET!
OHMYGOSH!
- - ON A SINKING CASKET!
IT'S GOING UNDER - -
I CAN'T BAIL FAST ENOUGH!

HUH.
IT'S SO QUIET DOWN HERE.
PEACEFUL.
SAY...
WHAT IS THAT?
uh, oh.
IT'S GETTING BIGGER!

WAIT! IT'S THE DRAGON!
I'M SAVED!
HEY! DRAGON! HERE I AM!
HE DOESN'T SEE ME.
I'M GOING INTO HIS MOUTH!

I CAN'T BELIEVE IT!
HE SWALLOWED ME.
NOW WHAT DID HE HAVE TO GO AND DO THAT FOR?

BONE
WHOA-- MAN!
WHAT A WEIRD DREAM I JUST HAD, SMILEY! I DREAMT I WAS SWALLOWED BY THE DRAGON --
SMILEY?
WHERE'D YOU GO?
HEY!
YO, FONE BONE! OVER HERE!

SMILEY! THERE YOU ARE. WHAT ARE YOU DOING?
TAKING A BATH! DO YOU REALIZE HOW LONG IT'S BEEN?
OH, THANK GOODNESS! I HAD THIS REALLY OMINOUS DREAM, AND I WAS AFRAID SOMETHING BAD MIGHT HAVE HAPPENED- -
WAIT!
WHAT'S WRONG?!
I DON'T HAVE ANY CLOTHES ON!
I'VE SEEN YOU WITHOUT YOUR VEST ON BEFORE. WE GREW UP TOGETHER, REMEMBER?
OKAY. YOU CAN COME IN NOW. I'M DECENT.
JEEZ. I CAN'T GET USED TO THIS EERIE LANDSCAPE. THE VOLCANO DID SO MUCH DAMAGE . . .
WHERE IS EVERYONE?
PHONEY'S RIGHT HERE.
AND LOOK! HE WOKE UP THIS MORNING AND HE'S NOT CAPTAIN AHAB ANYMORE! ISN'T THAT WEIRD?

SAY. . . I'M NOT DRESSED LIKE ISHMAEL ANYMORE, EITHER! WHAT'S GOING ON?
MAYBE THE VOLCANIC GASES THAT WERE MAKING US HALLUCINATE ARE STARTING TO WEAR OFF.
WAIT A MINUTE! IN MY DREAM I WAS DRESSED LIKE ISHMAEL UNTIL THE GREAT RED DRAGON SWALLOWED ME!
DO YOU THINK THAT MEANS ANYTHING?
THAT YOU'RE A PSYCHO?
WHERE'S THORN?
I THINK SOMETHING'S WRONG - -
I CAN FEEL IT. SOMETHING'S STARTING TO CHANGE . . .
TAKE IT EASY, WILL YA?
I'M SERIOUS, PHONEY, WHERE'S THORN? I THINK SHE'S IN DANGER!
SHE'S JUST ON THE OTHER SIDE OF THE TREE. WOULD YOU RELAX?
WHERE?
COME ON, I'LL SHOW YOU.
SEE? SHE'S FINE!

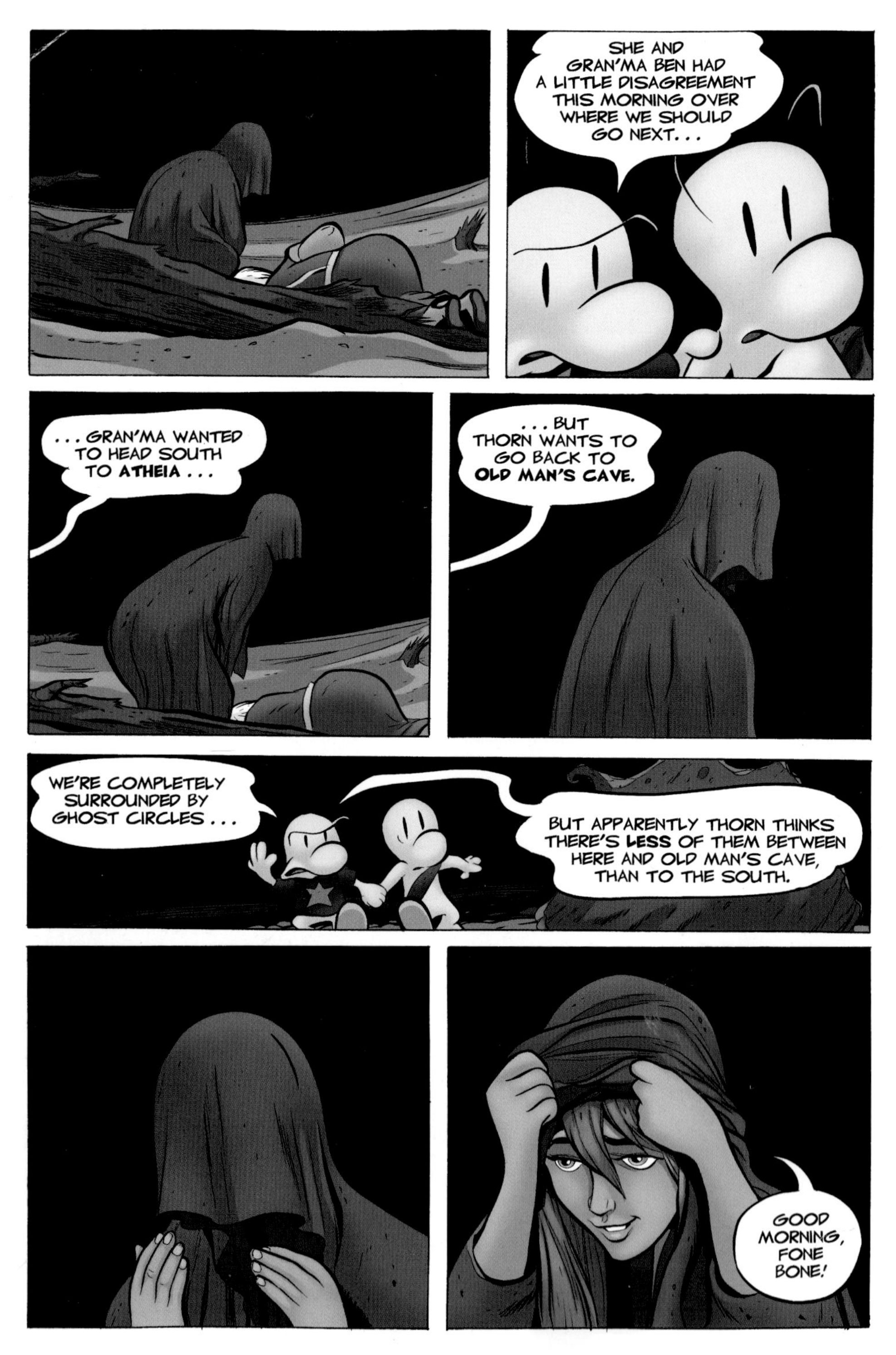
SHE AND GRAN'MA BEN HAD A LITTLE DISAGREEMENT THIS MORNING OVER WHERE WE SHOULD GO NEXT...
...GRAN'MA WANTED TO HEAD SOUTH TO ATHEIA...
...BUT THORN WANTS TO GO BACK TO OLD MAN'S CAVE.
WE'RE COMPLETELY SURROUNDED BY GHOST CIRCLES...
BUT APPARENTLY THORN THINKS THERE'S LESS OF THEM BETWEEN HERE AND OLD MAN'S CAVE, THAN TO THE SOUTH.
GOOD MORNING, FONE BONE!

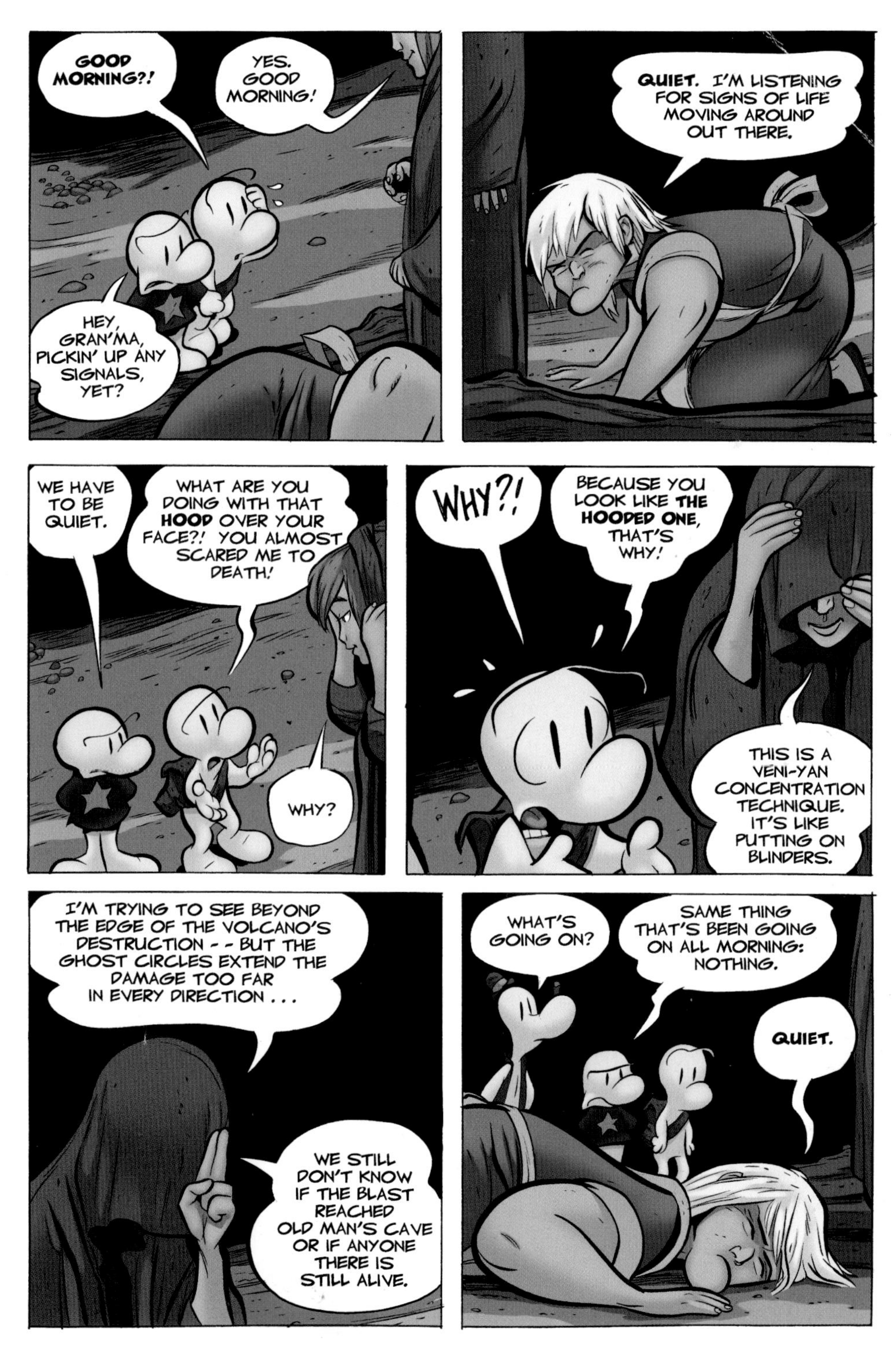
GOOD MORNING?!
YES. GOOD MORNING!
HEY, GRAN'MA, PICKIN' UP ANY SIGNALS, YET?
QUIET. I'M LISTENING FOR SIGNS OF LIFE MOVING AROUND OUT THERE.
WE HAVE TO BE QUIET.
WHAT ARE YOU DOING WITH THAT HOOD OVER YOUR FACE?! YOU ALMOST SCARED ME TO DEATH!
WHY?
WHY?!
BECAUSE YOU LOOK LIKE THE HOODED ONE, THAT'S WHY!
THIS IS A VENI-YAN CONCENTRATION TECHNIQUE. IT'S LIKE PUTTING ON BLINDERS.
I'M TRYING TO SEE BEYOND THE EDGE OF THE VOLCANO'S DESTRUCTION - - BUT THE GHOST CIRCLES EXTEND THE DAMAGE TOO FAR IN EVERY DIRECTION . . .
WE STILL DON'T KNOW IF THE BLAST REACHED OLD MAN'S CAVE OR IF ANYONE THERE IS STILL ALIVE.
WHAT'S GOING ON?
SAME THING THAT'S BEEN GOING ON ALL MORNING: NOTHING.
QUIET.

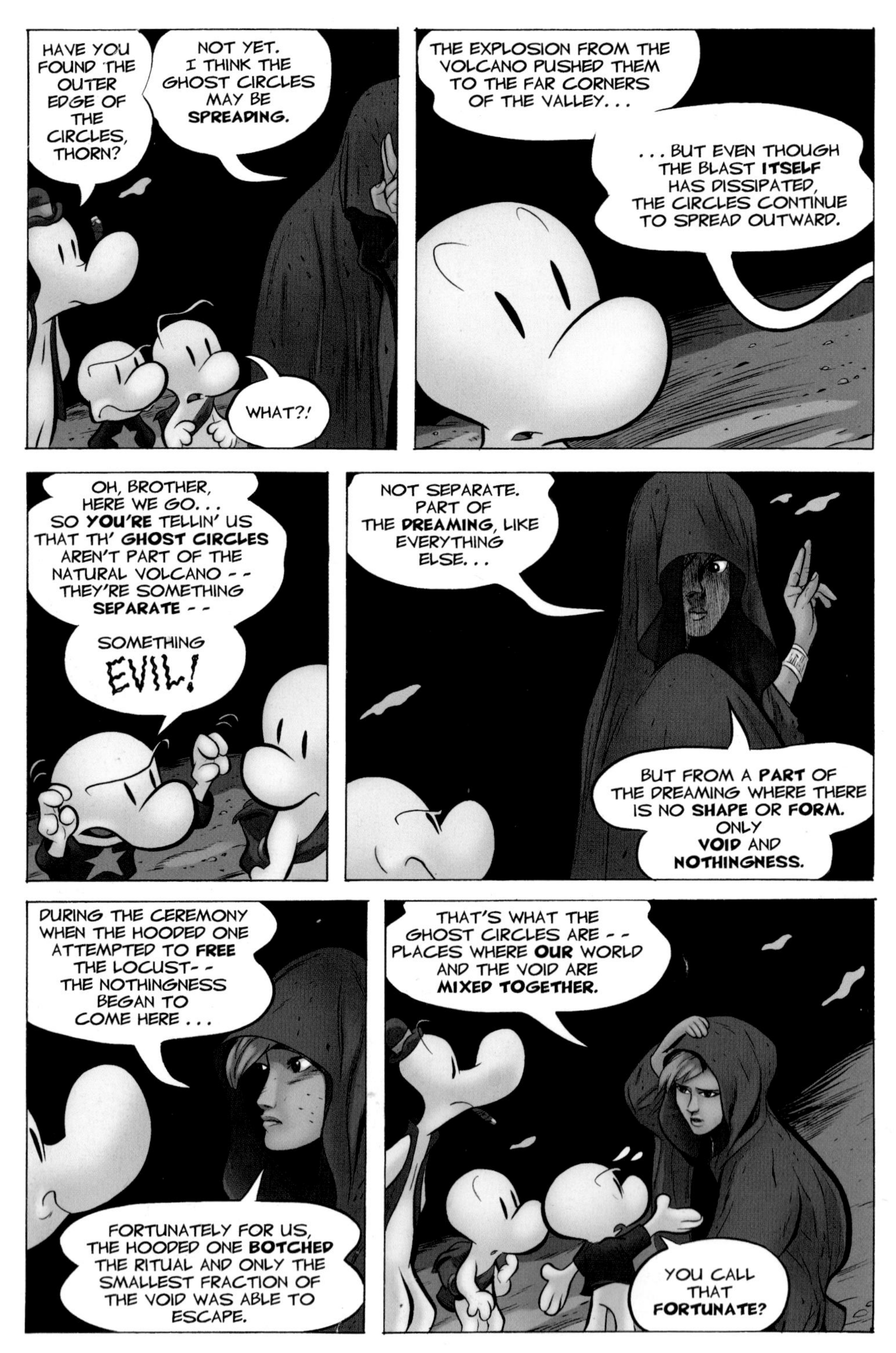
HAVE YOU FOUND THE OUTER EDGE OF THE CIRCLES, THORN?
NOT YET. I THINK THE GHOST CIRCLES MAY BE SPREADING.
WHAT?!
THE EXPLOSION FROM THE VOLCANO PUSHED THEM TO THE FAR CORNERS OF THE VALLEY...
...BUT EVEN THOUGH THE BLAST ITSELF HAS DISSIPATED, THE CIRCLES CONTINUE TO SPREAD OUTWARD.
OH, BROTHER, HERE WE GO... SO YOU'RE TELLIN' US THAT TH' GHOST CIRCLES AREN'T PART OF THE NATURAL VOLCANO -- THEY'RE SOMETHING SEPARATE --
SOMETHING EVIL!
NOT SEPARATE. PART OF THE DREAMING, LIKE EVERYTHING ELSE...
BUT FROM A PART OF THE DREAMING WHERE THERE IS NO SHAPE OR FORM. ONLY VOID AND NOTHINGNESS.
DURING THE CEREMONY WHEN THE HOODED ONE ATTEMPTED TO FREE THE LOCUST-- THE NOTHINGNESS BEGAN TO COME HERE...
FORTUNATELY FOR US, THE HOODED ONE BOTCHED THE RITUAL AND ONLY THE SMALLEST FRACTION OF THE VOID WAS ABLE TO ESCAPE.
THAT'S WHAT THE GHOST CIRCLES ARE -- PLACES WHERE OUR WORLD AND THE VOID ARE MIXED TOGETHER.
YOU CALL THAT FORTUNATE?

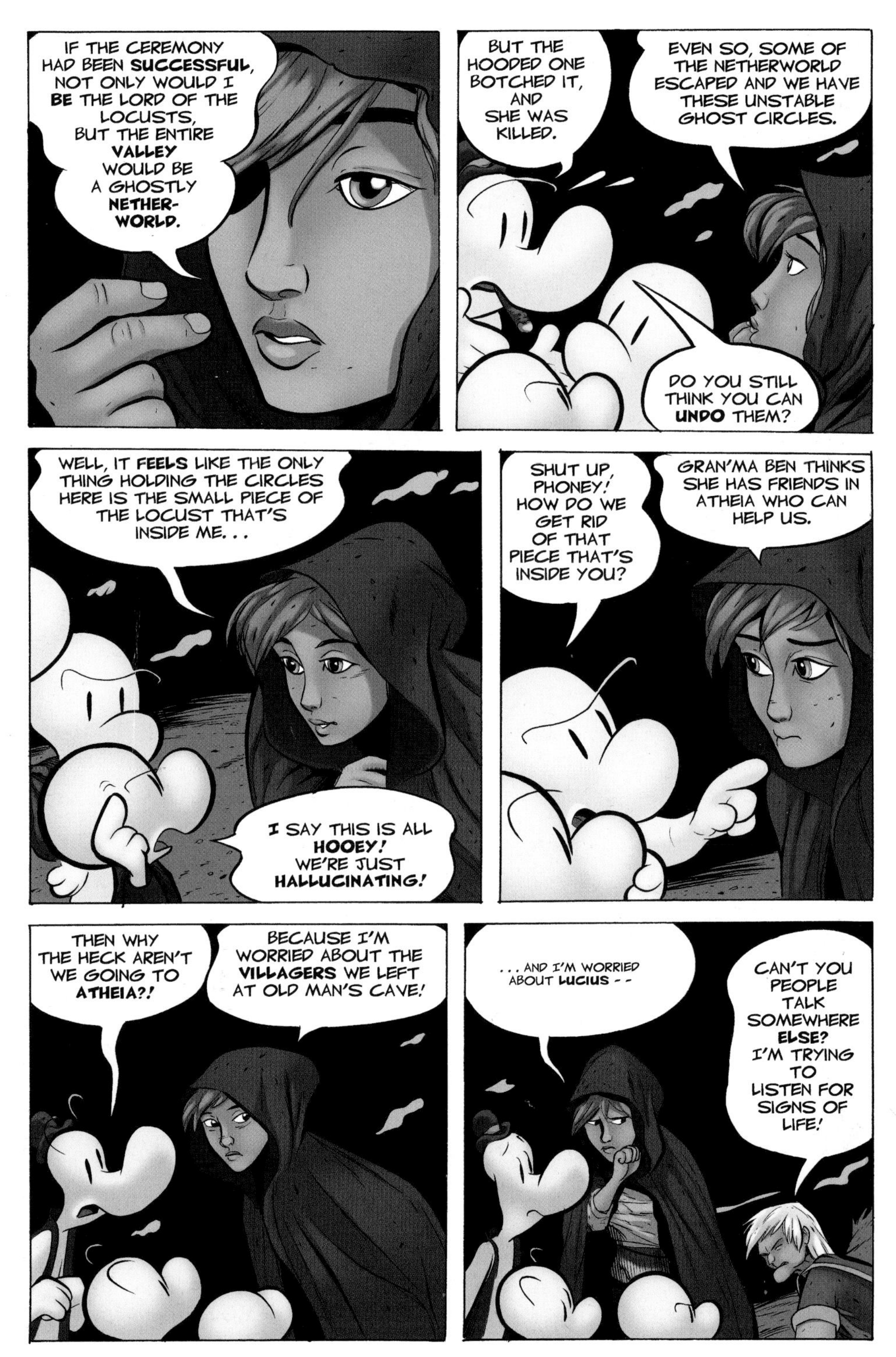
IF THE CEREMONY HAD BEEN SUCCESSFUL, NOT ONLY WOULD I BE THE LORD OF THE LOCUSTS, BUT THE ENTIRE VALLEY WOULD BE A GHOSTLY NETHER-WORLD.
BUT THE HOODED ONE BOTCHED IT, AND SHE WAS KILLED.
EVEN SO, SOME OF THE NETHERWORLD ESCAPED AND WE HAVE THESE UNSTABLE GHOST CIRCLES.
DO YOU STILL THINK YOU CAN UNDO THEM?
WELL, IT FEELS LIKE THE ONLY THING HOLDING THE CIRCLES HERE IS THE SMALL PIECE OF THE LOCUST THAT'S INSIDE ME...
I SAY THIS IS ALL HOOEY! WE'RE JUST HALLUCINATING!
SHUT UP, PHONEY! HOW DO WE GET RID OF THAT PIECE THAT'S INSIDE YOU?
GRAN'MA BEN THINKS SHE HAS FRIENDS IN ATHEIA WHO CAN HELP US.
THEN WHY THE HECK AREN'T WE GOING TO ATHEIA?!
BECAUSE I'M WORRIED ABOUT THE VILLAGERS WE LEFT AT OLD MAN'S CAVE!
...AND I'M WORRIED ABOUT LUCIUS --
CAN'T YOU PEOPLE TALK SOMEWHERE ELSE? I'M TRYING TO LISTEN FOR SIGNS OF LIFE!

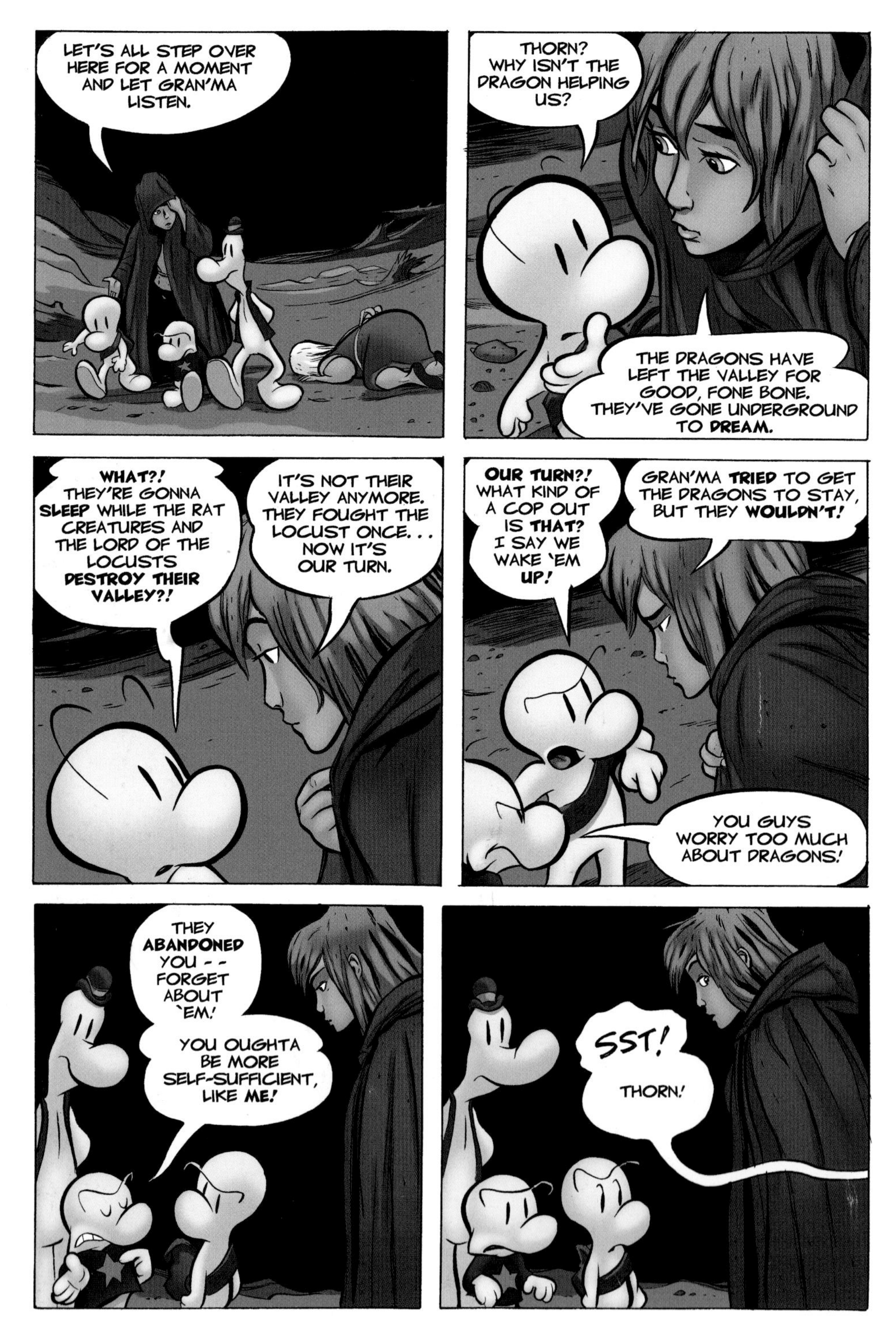
LET'S ALL STEP OVER HERE FOR A MOMENT AND LET GRAN'MA LISTEN.
THORN? WHY ISN'T THE DRAGON HELPING US?
THE DRAGONS HAVE LEFT THE VALLEY FOR GOOD, FONE BONE. THEY'VE GONE UNDERGROUND TO DREAM.
WHAT?! THEY'RE GONNA SLEEP WHILE THE RAT CREATURES AND THE LORD OF THE LOCUSTS DESTROY THEIR VALLEY?!
IT'S NOT THEIR VALLEY ANYMORE. THEY FOUGHT THE LOCUST ONCE. . . NOW IT'S OUR TURN.
OUR TURN?! WHAT KIND OF A COP OUT IS THAT? I SAY WE WAKE 'EM UP!
GRAN'MA TRIED TO GET THE DRAGONS TO STAY, BUT THEY WOULDN'T!
YOU GUYS WORRY TOO MUCH ABOUT DRAGONS!
THEY ABANDONED YOU - - FORGET ABOUT 'EM!
YOU OUGHTA BE MORE SELF-SUFFICIENT, LIKE ME!
SST!
THORN!

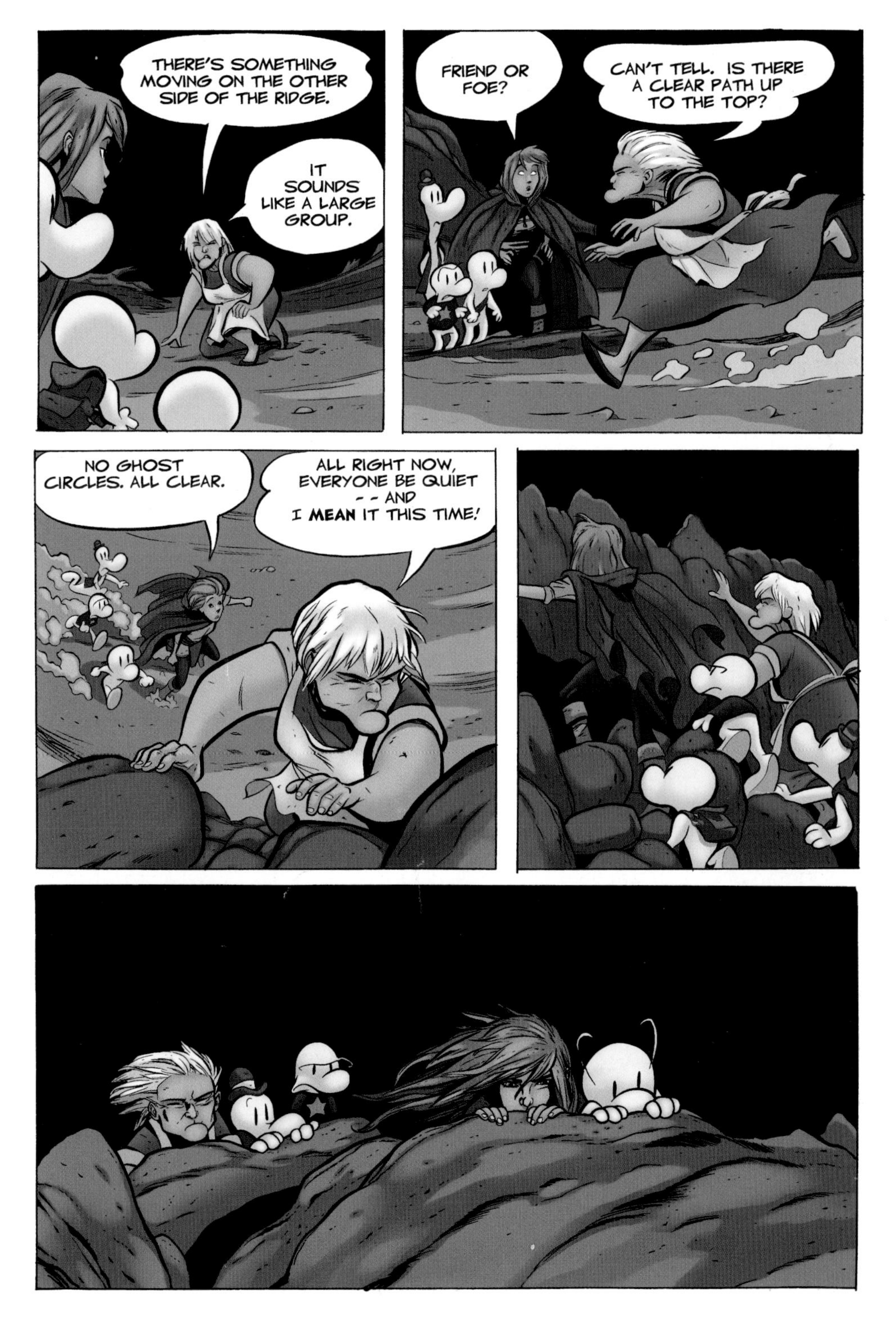
THERE'S SOMETHING MOVING ON THE OTHER SIDE OF THE RIDGE.
IT SOUNDS LIKE A LARGE GROUP.
FRIEND OR FOE?
CAN'T TELL. IS THERE A CLEAR PATH UP TO THE TOP?
NO GHOST CIRCLES. ALL CLEAR.
ALL RIGHT NOW, EVERYONE BE QUIET - - AND I MEAN IT THIS TIME!

OH, NO.
RAT CREATURES! HOW DID THEY FIND US?
THEY DON'T KNOW WE'RE HERE.
COME ON, LET'S GET BACK BEFORE THEY SEE US.

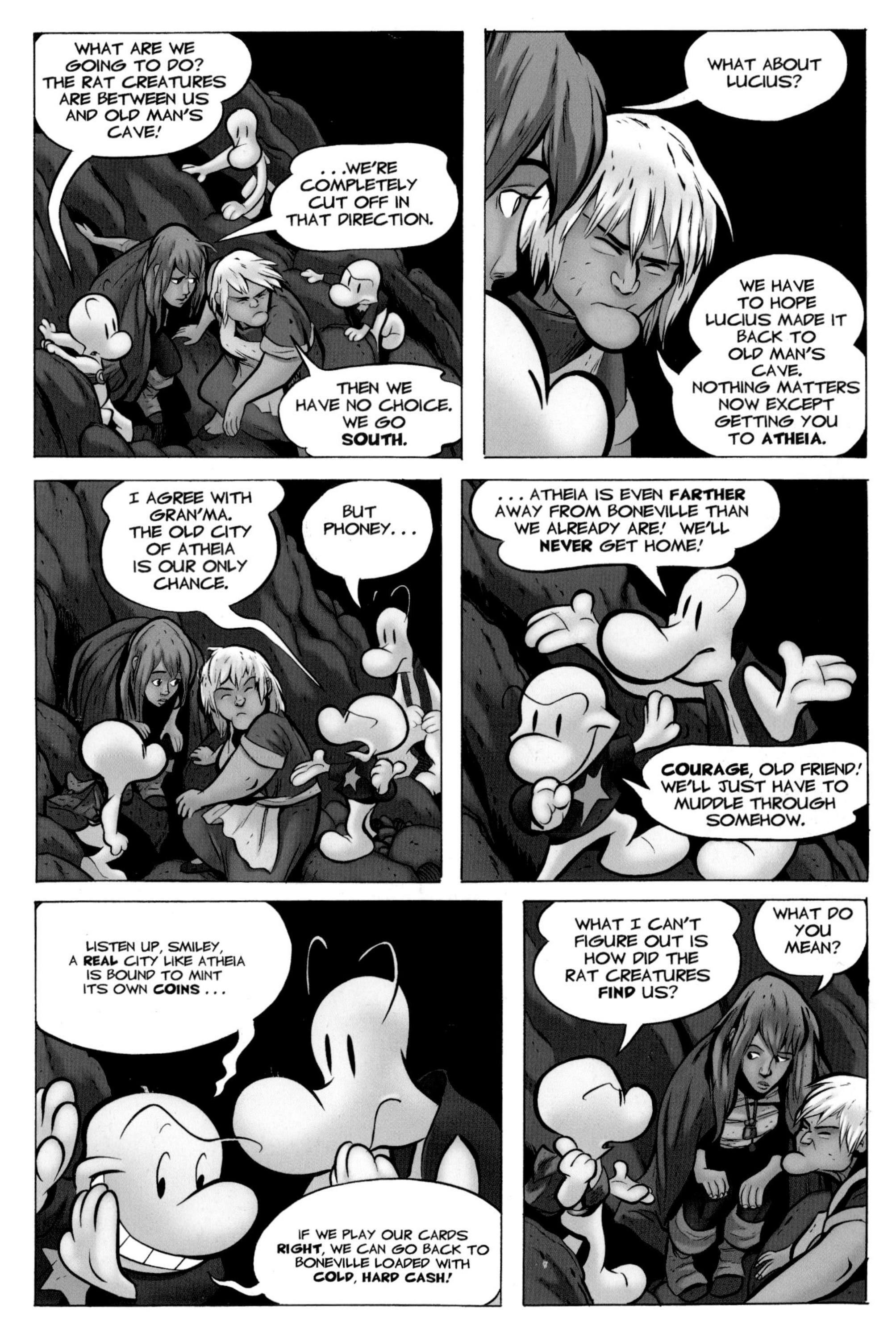
WHAT ARE WE GOING TO DO? THE RAT CREATURES ARE BETWEEN US AND OLD MAN'S CAVE!
. . .WE'RE COMPLETELY CUT OFF IN THAT DIRECTION.
THEN WE HAVE NO CHOICE. WE GO SOUTH.
WHAT ABOUT LUCIUS?
WE HAVE TO HOPE LUCIUS MADE IT BACK TO OLD MAN'S CAVE. NOTHING MATTERS NOW EXCEPT GETTING YOU TO ATHEIA.
I AGREE WITH GRAN'MA. THE OLD CITY OF ATHEIA IS OUR ONLY CHANCE.
BUT PHONEY. . .
. . . ATHEIA IS EVEN FARTHER AWAY FROM BONEVILLE THAN WE ALREADY ARE! WE'LL NEVER GET HOME!
COURAGE, OLD FRIEND! WE'LL JUST HAVE TO MUDDLE THROUGH SOMEHOW.
LISTEN UP, SMILEY, A REAL CITY LIKE ATHEIA IS BOUND TO MINT ITS OWN COINS . . .
IF WE PLAY OUR CARDS RIGHT, WE CAN GO BACK TO BONEVILLE LOADED WITH COLD, HARD CASH!
WHAT I CAN'T FIGURE OUT IS HOW DID THE RAT CREATURES FIND US?
WHAT DO YOU MEAN?

YOU THINK IT'S A COINCIDENCE THAT THEY MARCHED ACROSS MILES AND MILES OF DEVASTATED LANDSCAPE TO WITHIN A FEW YARDS OF OUR CAMP?
OHMYGOSH! MAYBE THEY DO KNOW WE'RE HERE.
HOW COULD THEY?
WHEN FONE BONE AND I DISTURBED THE GHOST CIRCLE - - THAT COULD'VE GIVEN US AWAY!
IMPOSSIBLE! WITHOUT BRIAR, THE RATS CAN'T SEE ANYTHING THAT HAPPENS IN THE DREAMING. AND BRIAR IS DEAD.
EVEN WITHOUT YOUR SISTER, SOMETHING GUIDED THOSE CREATURES HERE.
MAYBE THEY SAW OUR CAMPFIRE LAST NIGHT.
I THINK WE SHOULD GET OUT OF HERE.
I AGREE. LET'S GO.

RUN, THORN!
THIS WAY!

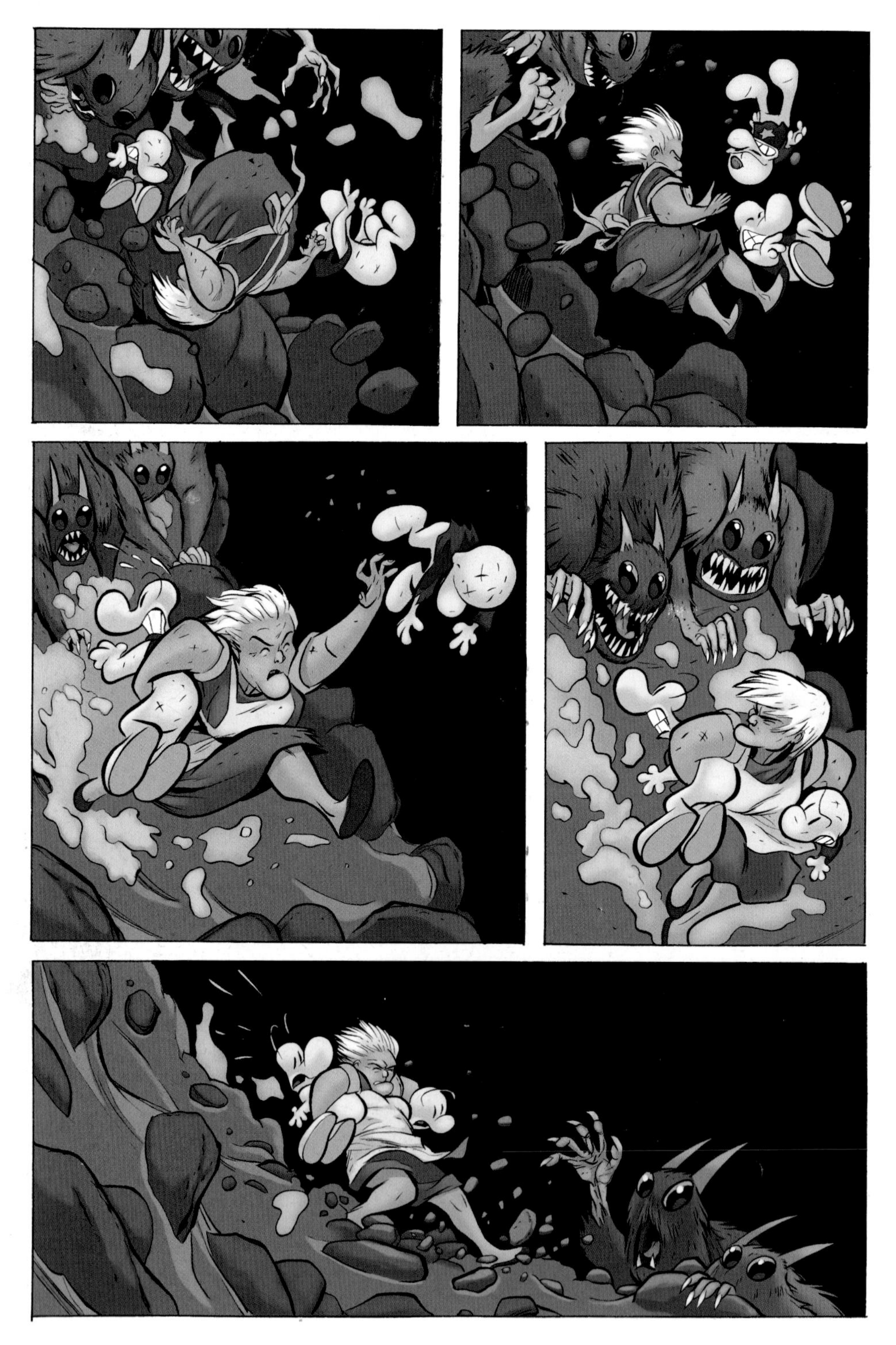

WE LOST THORN . . .
EVERYONE PUT YOUR BACKS TOGETHER!
STICK WITH ME . . .
I'M GOING TO PUNCH THROUGH THE WEAKEST POINT IN THEIR RANKS - -
WAIT!
HOLD ON A MINUTE - -

Huff! Huff!
HOW MUCH FARTHER CAN WE GO?
NOWHERE --
IT'S STRAIGHT DOWN!

GET BACK!
AAARR!
SNIK!
POW
STOP....
STAY AWAY FROM US - -
OR I'LL KILL YOU ...
I HAVE POWERS NOW THAT YOU CAN ONLY IMAGINE ...
CHILD ...
I AM ALREADY DEAD .....
AND YOU CERTAINLY WILL DO NO DAMAGE TO ME WITH THAT TINY BLADE ...

NOW THIS . . .
THIS IS
A
BLADE.

ANY POWER YOU HAVE COMES TO YOU FROM THE LOCUST HIMSELF...... YOU DID NOT STEAL IT... ...HE GAVE IT TO YOU....
YOU ARE LIKE ME NOW.... A SHADOW OF YOUR MASTER...
A SHADOW CAST INTO THIS WORLD.
BUT THERE IS A DIFFERENCE BETWEEN YOU AND I... A DIFFERENCE THAT WILL ALLOW US TO FREE THE LORD OF THE LOCUSTS...
W--WHAT?
YOU ARE ALIVE.
BUT EVEN A LIVING VEN-YAN-CARI CANNOT CALL OUT THE LOCUST ALONE... TWO TOGETHER ARE NECESSARY TO PERFORM THE RITUAL...
I HAD HOPED TO BE THE STRONGER OF THE TWO BUT IT WAS NOT MEANT TO BE...
COME WITH ME, CHILD... WE WILL GO TO PERFORM THE RITUAL TOGETHER...
GO AWAY.

DO NOT DECIDE TOO QUICKLY . . . WITH THE POWER OF THE LOCUST YOU WILL BE ABLE TO UNDO THE GHOST CIRCLES . . . YOU CAN RESTORE THE VALLEY . . . IS THAT NOT WHAT YOU WANT?
I KNOW WHO YOU ARE, BRIAR.
I KNOW IT WAS YOU WHO TOLD THE RAT CREATURES WHERE TO FIND MY MOTHER AND FATHER SO YOU COULD KILL THEM!
IT WAS NOT I WHO KILLED YOUR PARENTS . . .
BUT THEY WHO KILLED ME . . . .
LIAR!
BUT IF I HAD, COULD YOU BLAME ME? YOUR ENTIRE FAMILY TREATED ME LIKE AN OLD NURSEMAID.
NO ONE KNEW I WAS A VENI-YAN-CARI LIKE YOU . . .
YES, I LED THEM TO THE RATS.
BUT WHEN YOUR MOTHER REALIZED I WAS KIDNAPPING YOU FOR THE RITUAL . . .
. . . YOUR FATHER CUT ME IN HALF WITH AN OLD ABANDONED FARM TOOL.
ONLY LATER DID I LEARN THAT YOUR PARENTS WERE EATEN ALIVE. . .
uhh...
THE WORLD IS FILLED WITH DARK TRUTHS, YOUNG ONE . . . AND ONE TRUTH I HAVE LEARNED IS DESTINY ALWAYS PREVAILS . . .
NOW RISE . . . TAKE MY HAND.
ON THE NEXT FULL MOON WE WILL PERFORM THE RITUAL . . .

YOU HAVE THE LOCUST INSIDE YOU NOW . . . IT CONTROLS YOU . . . IT WILL NOT ALLOW YOU TO RESIST . . .
SPLAT!
YOU KNOW WHAT? I HAVE JUST ABOUT HAD IT WITH YOU.
FIRST YOU MESSED WITH MY COUSIN, NOW YOU'RE MESSIN' WITH MY GIRL!
LET'S GO - -
RIGHT NOW!
THERE IS A PIECE OF THE LOCUST INSIDE OF YOU AS WELL . . .
WHAT?

. . . HEH . . .
HEH . . . HEH . .
FROM THE VERY BEGINNING THE DREAMS SHOWED ME THAT A BONE CREATURE WOULD BECOME INVOLVED IN THIS AFFAIR . . .
. . . I JUST HAD THE WRONG ONE . . .
HEH HEH. . .
HOWEVER, SINCE THIS BONE WOULD CLEARLY BE A WEAKER PARTNER . . .
. . . THAT MEANS I NO LONGER NEED YOU, PRINCESS - -
LOOK OUT!

YAH! YAH! GOOD ONE, BARTLEBY! QUICK-- GO BACK!
SCREECH!
HIYA, FONE BONE!
REMEMBER BARTLEBY? HE HELPED PHONEY, GRAN'MA BEN AN' ME GET AWAY!
GO! GO! GET THORN ON THAT RAT CREATURE AND RIDE!
WHAT ABOUT THE GHOST CIRCLES?
I CAN GUIDE YOU.

CAN YOU BELIEVE IT, FONE BONE? OUR LITTLE BARTLEBY'S BACK!
AN' LOOK HOW HE'S GROWN!
MESSIN' WITH YOUR GIRL, HUH?
oh, JEEZ...

BONE
WHICH WAY, THORN?
GO TO THE LEFT! THERE ARE GHOST CIRCLES AHEAD - -
TO THE LEFT! CAN'T YOU STEER THIS THING?
THE GHOST CIRCLES ARE INVISIBLE! ONLY YOU CAN SEE THEM!
YOU'RE GOING TO KILL US! SLOW DOWN!
SLOW DOWN!
SPEED UP! SPEED UP!

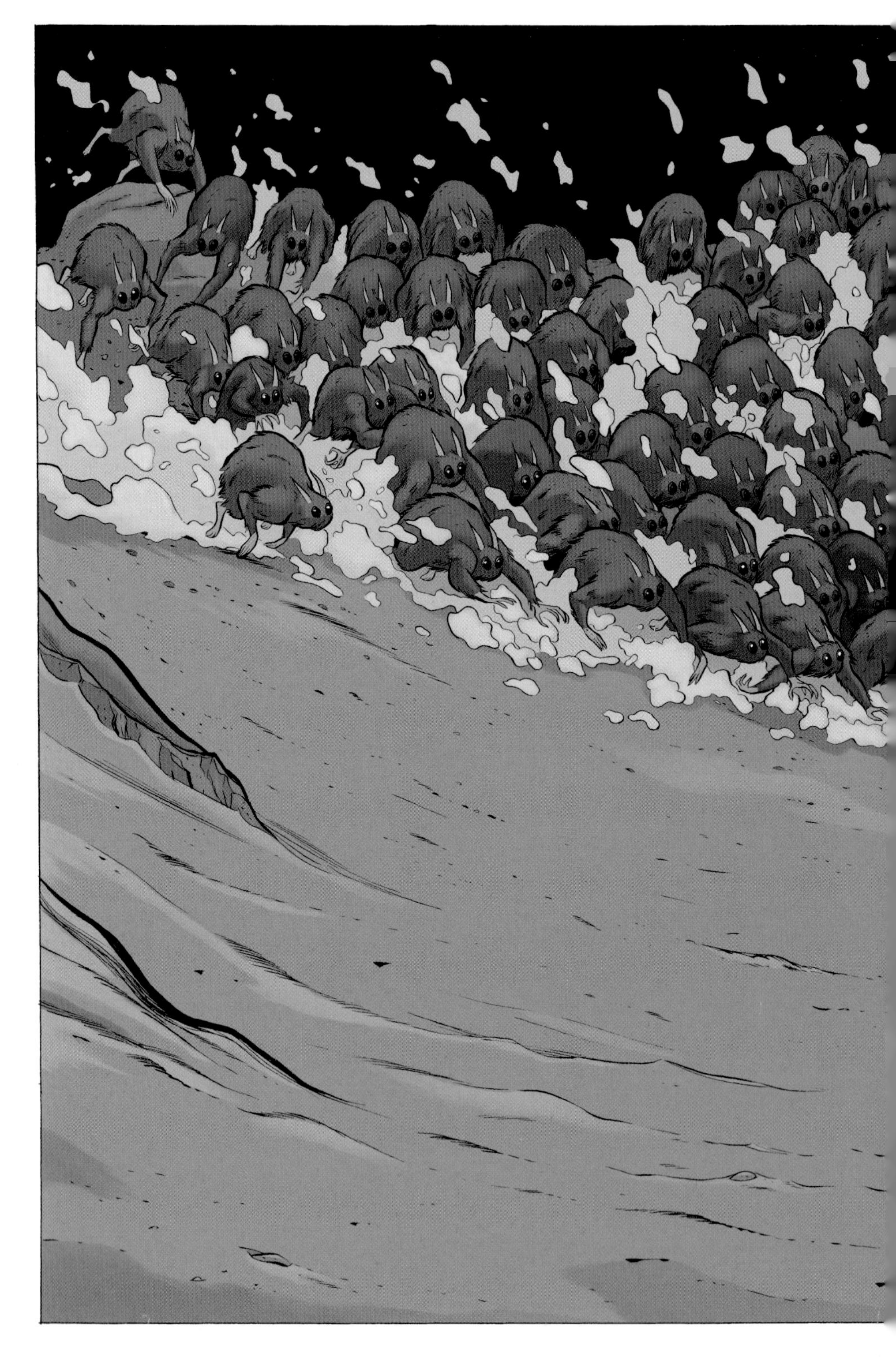

FONE BONE! GRAN'MA! LISTEN TO ME!
THIS IS ABOUT TO GET REAL DANGEROUS!
WE'RE ENTERING A MASSIVE FIELD OF GHOST CIRCLES!
!

AAIEE--
ZFFT!
AAAH!
YIIII!
AAA
THE RAT CREATURES ARE DISAPPEARING!
DON'T LOOK!
AAAIEE!
AAH!
SINGLE FILE! GO SLOW!
PPF
FFF
SHRRRAK!
PFFT!
AAEE

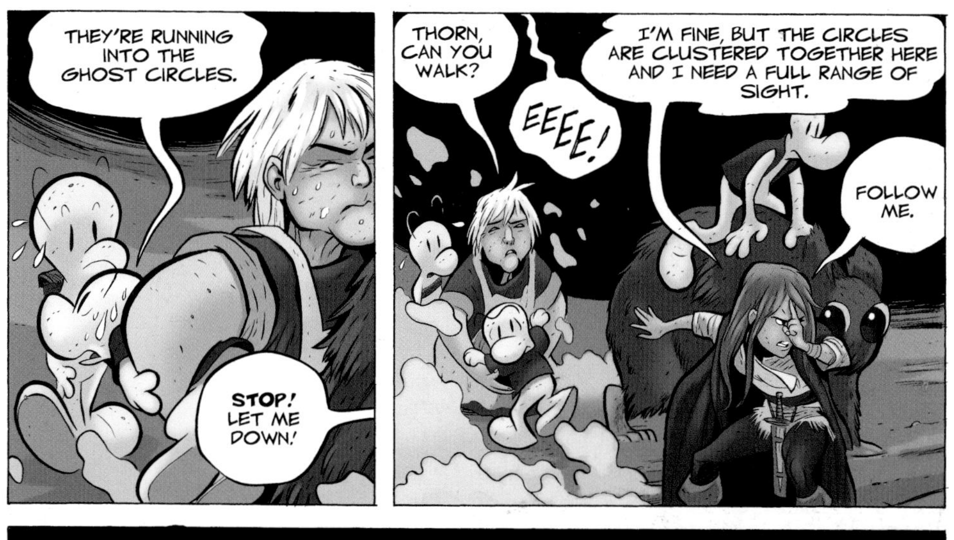
THEY'RE RUNNING INTO THE GHOST CIRCLES.
STOP! LET ME DOWN!
THORN, CAN YOU WALK?
EEEE!
I'M FINE, BUT THE CIRCLES ARE CLUSTERED TOGETHER HERE AND I NEED A FULL RANGE OF SIGHT.
FOLLOW ME.

THEY STOPPED YELLING.
MUST'VE TURNED BACK.

WE CAN STOP HERE FOR A MOMENT. I NEED TO REST.
THANK YOU, BARTLEBY.
WHAT A WORLD.
BRIAR IS STILL ALIVE . . .
. . . AND EVERYONE ELSE EXCEPT US IS DEAD.
UM.....
I THINK WE SHOULD KEEP MOVING.
WE'RE NOT SAFE YET, SO LET'S KEEP HEADING SOUTH.

GO ON, THORN, SHOW US THE WAY.

WENDELL!
WE FOUND LUCIUS! HE'S ALIVE!
THANK THE STARS!
IT'S A MIRACLE THAT WE FOUND HIM!
WHERE WAS HE?
IN CONKLE'S HOLLOW. . . . . . I KEPT FOLLOWIN' A QUEER BUZZIN' SOUND IN MY EAR.
. . . FOR THE LIFE OF ME, I'LL NEVER KNOW WHAT MADE ME LOOK THERE.

LUCIUS? CAN YOU HEAR ME?
WENDELL - - ?
YOU'RE SAFE, BUDDY. YOU'RE GOING TO BE ALL RIGHT.
DON'T REMEMBER MUCH AFTER TH' BLAST...
IS JONATHAN HERE?
YEAH...
YEAH, HE'S GOOD - - HE'S HERE. DON'T THINK ABOUT THAT RIGHT NOW.
WHY AREN'T YOU LOOKIN' ME IN THE EYE, WENDELL? WHAT HAPPENED?
NO.
NOT JONATHAN.
oh... hhhf...
DON'T MOVE. WE'RE GOING TO GET YOU CLEANED UP...
IT'S ALL MY FAULT, WENDELL!
IT'S ALL MY FAULT!

I WOULDN'T SHOUT THAT IF I WERE YOU, FRIEND.
THERE'S PLENTY AROUND HERE LOOKIN' TO PIN BLAME - -
SST.
HEADS UP.
HERE COMES THE HEADMASTER.
STAND ASIDE, FARMER.
DON'T GET UP, LUCIUS.
WHERE ARE THEY?
YOU MEAN ROSE?
YES, THE QUEEN MOTHER AND HER GRANDDAUGHTER.
WHERE ARE THEY?
IF THEY'RE NOT HERE, THEN I DON'T KNOW.

SHE WAS LAST SEEN WITH YOU AND A BONE CREATURE HEADING TOWARD THE MOUNTAIN. . .
. . .THE MOUNTAIN THAT HAS SINCE EXPLODED, FREEING THE LORD OF THE LOCUSTS.
I DON'T THINK YOU AND I WOULD BE ALIVE IF THE LOCUST WAS TRULY FREE.
AND IF WE'RE ALIVE, THEN MAYBE ROSE, THORN AND THE BONES ARE, TOO.
I KNOW IF ROSE SURVIVED, THEN SHE IS GOING SOUTH. . . TAKING THORN TO ATHEIA.
TO WHAT END? THE ANCIENT CAPITAL WENT DARK YEARS AGO. THERE IS NOTHING LEFT.
IT'S THE SEAT OF THE THRONE. SHE AND THORN ARE GOING TO REUNITE OUR PEOPLE AGAINST THE ENEMY.
WE SHOULD GO, TOO.
IMMEDIATELY.
NO.
THE ONLY SURVIVORS OF THIS DISASTER ARE THE MEMBERS OF OUR ORDER AND YOUR VILLAGERS WHO WERE IN THE CAVE WITH US.
THE WAR IS OVER AND WE LOST.

YOU DON'T KNOW THAT. THERE COULD BE OTHER SURVIVORS - -
WE DO NOT SHARE YOUR OPTIMISTIC VIEW.
THE LOCUST IS FREE, AND THE END TIMES ARE UPON US.
WE WILL DO WHATEVER WE MUST TO PRESERVE OUR WAY OF LIFE.
SHING
TAKE LUCIUS TO THE INFIRMARY AND PLACE A GUARD AROUND HIM.
HE IS A TRAITOR TO THE QUEEN.
SHING! SHING! SHING!

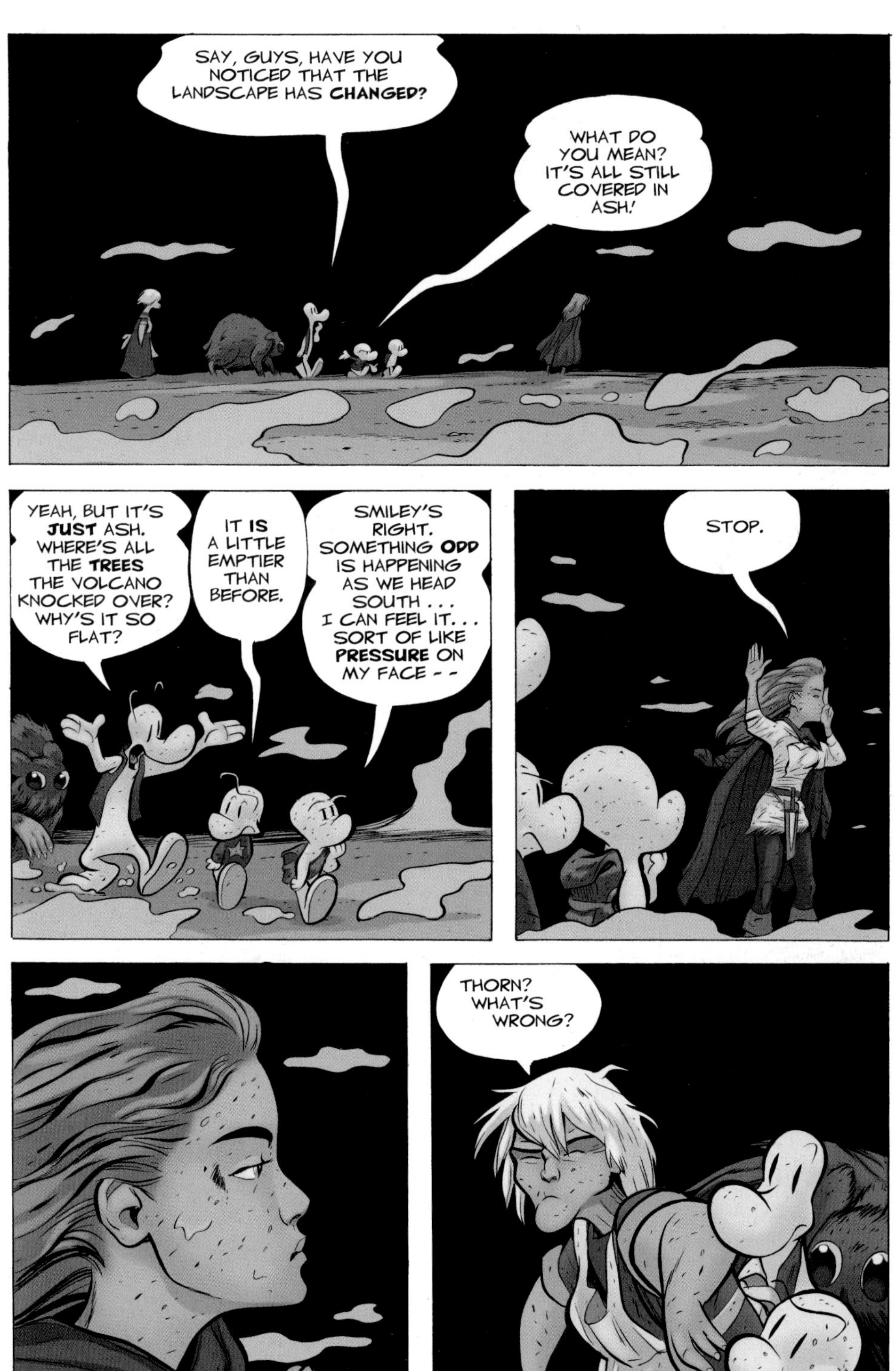
SAY, GUYS, HAVE YOU NOTICED THAT THE LANDSCAPE HAS CHANGED?
WHAT DO YOU MEAN? IT'S ALL STILL COVERED IN ASH!
YEAH, BUT IT'S JUST ASH. WHERE'S ALL THE TREES THE VOLCANO KNOCKED OVER? WHY'S IT SO FLAT?
IT IS A LITTLE EMPTIER THAN BEFORE.
SMILEY'S RIGHT. SOMETHING ODD IS HAPPENING AS WE HEAD SOUTH . . . I CAN FEEL IT. . . SORT OF LIKE PRESSURE ON MY FACE - -
STOP.
THORN? WHAT'S WRONG?

IT'S STRANGE, GRAN'MA. . . THE GHOST CIRCLES SHOULD BE THINNING OUT AS WE GET FARTHER FROM THE MOUNTAIN, BUT INSTEAD THEY SEEM TO BE GROWING HEAVIER UP AHEAD.
IT'S ALMOST AS IF WE'VE MET A NEW SYSTEM OF GHOST CIRCLES MOVING UP FROM THE SOUTH TOWARDS US.
BLOODY STARS.
YET OFF TO THE EAST TOWARD PAWA, THERE'S A NARROW REGION FREE FROM ANY GHOST CIRCLES WHATSOEVER.
HMM.
OKAY, BREAK TIME.
WE AIN'T GOIN' ANYWHERE FAST.

SIT DOWN, WILL YA?
JEEZ, LOOK AT THE FACE.
WE'RE IN A PRETTY BAD SPOT, PHONEY.
AAH!
YOU WORRY TOO MUCH.
WHA - - ?
WORRY TOO MUCH? THE WORLD IS GOING AWAY!
IT'S JUST AN ASH PLUME. IT'LL BLOW OVER.
LOOK, ONCE WE GET TO THIS CITY OF ATHEIA EVERYTHING'S GONNA BE FINE . . .
SNAP!
. . . IT'S GONNA BE SO FINE, IN FACT, THAT YOU AN' I ARE GONNA BE ON EASY STREET!
OUCH!
SORRY!
I DIDN'T MEAN TO SHOCK YOU!
!
EASY STREET? DON'T TELL ME YOU'RE UP TO SOMETHING - - AGAIN?!!
GET OFF YOUR HIGH HORSE! YOU'VE BEEN BLAMING ME FOR OUR TROUBLES EVER SINCE WE GOT HERE, BUT I GUESS WE KNOW WHO'S TO BLAME NOW, DON'T WE?
SNAP!
YIIII!
WHO?
ARE YOU SAYING THIS IS MY FAULT?!

WELL, YOU'RE CRAZY!
ALL THIS TIME YOU BEEN MAKIN' SUCH A BIG DEAL ABOUT THE RAT CREATURES CHASIN' ME - -
YEEE!
SO?
SNAP!
SO THOSE DAYS ARE GONE - -
AAH!
CRACK!
WHOA! HEY!
SNAP!
SNAP CRACK
SMILEY! CUT IT OUT!
WE DON'T HAVE TIME TO PLAY AROUND!
THERE'S ALWAYS TIME FOR SCIENCE.
LISTEN UP, CHUMLY, THIS IS YOUR FAULT BECAUSE YOU HAVE A PIECE OF THE LOCUST INSIDE YOU, AND THAT MEANS THE RAT CREATURES WANT YOU . . .
. . . NOT ME, AND NOT SMILEY. . .
- - THEY DON'T EVEN WANT THORN ANYMORE - -
JUST YOU.

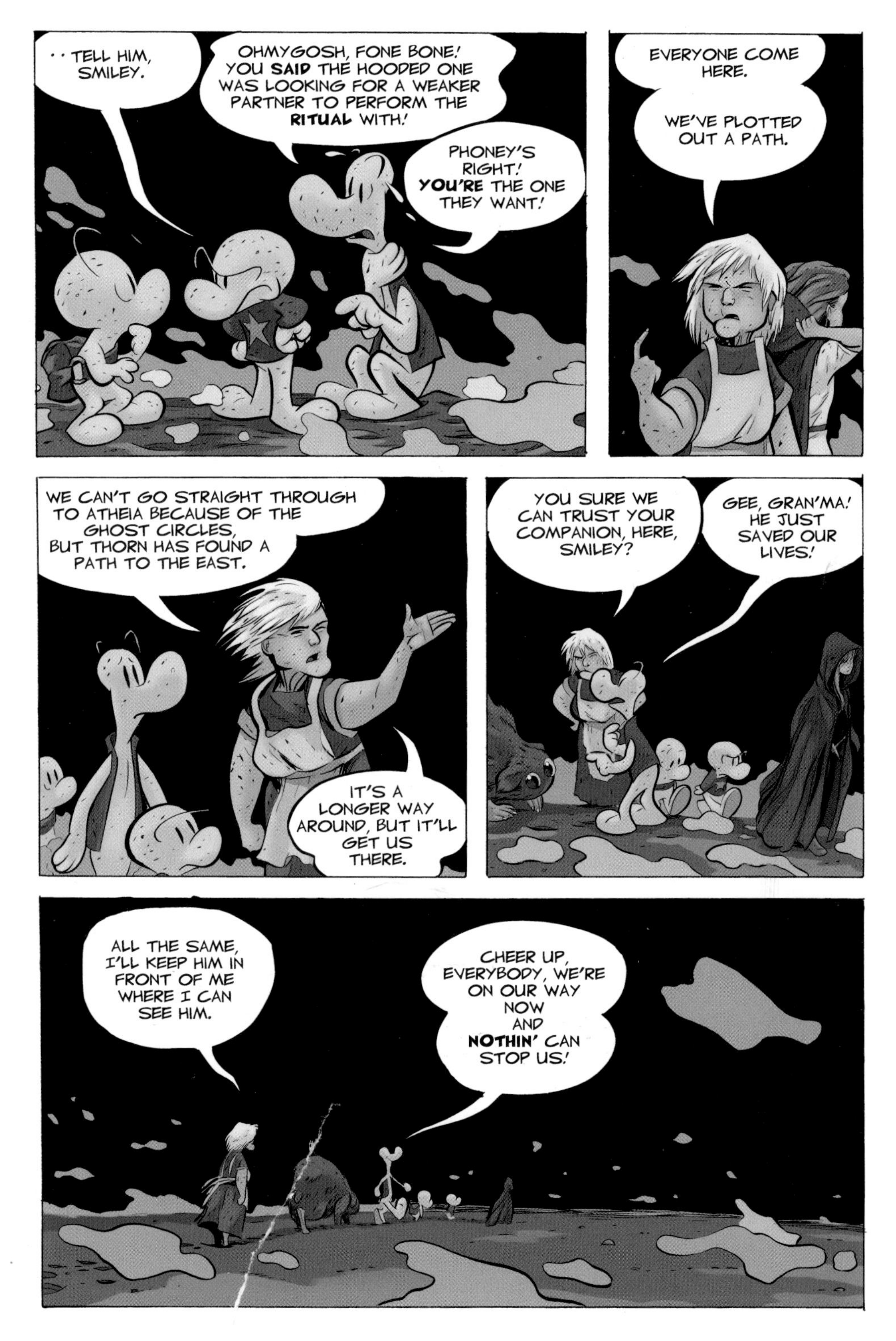

· · TELL HIM, SMILEY.
OHMYGOSH, FONE BONE! YOU SAID THE HOODED ONE WAS LOOKING FOR A WEAKER PARTNER TO PERFORM THE RITUAL WITH!
PHONEY'S RIGHT! YOU'RE THE ONE THEY WANT!
EVERYONE COME HERE.
WE'VE PLOTTED OUT A PATH.
WE CAN'T GO STRAIGHT THROUGH TO ATHEIA BECAUSE OF THE GHOST CIRCLES, BUT THORN HAS FOUND A PATH TO THE EAST.
IT'S A LONGER WAY AROUND, BUT IT'LL GET US THERE.
YOU SURE WE CAN TRUST YOUR COMPANION, HERE, SMILEY?
GEE, GRAN'MA! HE JUST SAVED OUR LIVES!
ALL THE SAME, I'LL KEEP HIM IN FRONT OF ME WHERE I CAN SEE HIM.
CHEER UP, EVERYBODY, WE'RE ON OUR WAY NOW AND NOTHIN' CAN STOP US!

BONE
BONE! BONE!
WHAT'S WRONG, BARTLEBY?
IT'S SMILEY! HE FELL!
OHMYGOSH.
BE CAREFUL! DON'T STEP INTO ANY GHOST CIRCLES!

SMILEY!

SMILEY! WHAT'S WRONG?
NEED...
TACO...

HE NEEDS FOOD. HE'S WEAK FROM HUNGER.
BUT I RATIONED OUT ALL THE STALE **BREAD THINGIES** IN MY BACKPACK- -

HE WOULDN'T EAT HIS RATIONS. HE INSISTED I EAT HIS SHARE.
oh, SMILEY...

I DON'T THINK WE HAVE ANY MORE . . .
HEY!

WHAT HAPPENED?
WHAT HAVE YOU DONE TO MY COUSIN?
HE COLLAPSED FROM HUNGER. JUST LIKE WE'RE ALL GOING TO IF WE DON'T FIND SOME FOOD SOON.
THORN! GET US SOMETHING -- QUICK, BEFORE SMILEY GETS WORSE!
ME? WHAT CAN I DO?
CAN'T YOU DO THE FINGERS-AGAINST-THE-FOREHEAD THING?
THE RIVERS ARE CHOKED WITH MUD AND YOU FOUND WATER...
WATER IS DIFFERENT. UNDERGROUND SPRINGS SURVIVED THE EXPLOSION.
ISN'T THERE SOME UNDERGROUND FOOD?
I'M SORRY, PHONEY. ANYTHING THAT WASN'T TRAPPED INSIDE A GHOST CIRCLE WAS DESTROYED.
THEN GO INSIDE A GHOST CIRCLE! THIS IS AN EMERGENCY!
SAY, WAIT A MINUTE...
YOU WANT ME TO GO INSIDE A GHOST CIRCLE?
NOT BY YOURSELF, BUT IF WE HELD HANDS LIKE BEFORE, MAYBE WE COULD GO INSIDE AND LOOK FOR A FARM OR A GARDEN...
I SUPPOSE WE COULD...

WHOA, WHOA!
I DIDN'T MEAN **YOU**, FONE BONE. WHY CAN'T THORN GO ALONE?
I HAVE A PIECE OF THE LOCUST INSIDE ME TOO.
BESIDES, I'M NOT GONNA LET HER TAKE ALL THE RISK!
WE'LL BE SAFE AS LONG AS WE HOLD HANDS. IT WORKED BEFORE.
IT WAS AN **ACCIDENT** BEFORE! HE'S NOT BUILT FOR DANGER THE WAY YOU ARE.
HEY!
GRAN'MA, WHERE ALONG THE RIVER ARE WE?
THE CIRCLES MAKE IT VERY CONFUSING, DEAR . . . WE MIGHT BE NEAR THE BANKS OF FLINT RIDGE - -
I DON'T WANT YOU TO DO THIS . . .
THAT MEANS WE'RE IN UPPER PAWA. THERE SHOULD BE FARMS ALL AROUND US.
GHOST CIRCLES ARE PART OF THE LOCUST HIMSELF. POISONOUS NIGHTMARES SENT FORTH TO DEMORALIZE AND CONTROL US.
LAST TIME YOU DID THIS, IT GAVE AWAY OUR POSITION TO THE ENEMY.
WE HAVE TO EAT.
THORN, I THINK THIS IS A **STRATEGIC ERROR** - -
PAWA IS **HOSTILE** TERRITORY. THE FARMERS HERE HAVE GONE OVER TO THE **LOCUST** - -
WHO CARES ABOUT THE STUPID **WAR**? WE'RE JUST TRYING TO **SURVIVE**!

FONE BONE! I THINK WE'RE ON A FARM NOW. . . . I'M DEFINITELY SENSING SOME OF THE OUT BUILDINGS.
LET'S GO BEFORE WE HAVE TIME TO THINK ABOUT IT.

OKAY. . . STEP RIGHT OVER HERE . . . THIS IS THE EDGE OF THE CIRCLE . . .
GOT MY HAND?
GOT IT.

STEP - -

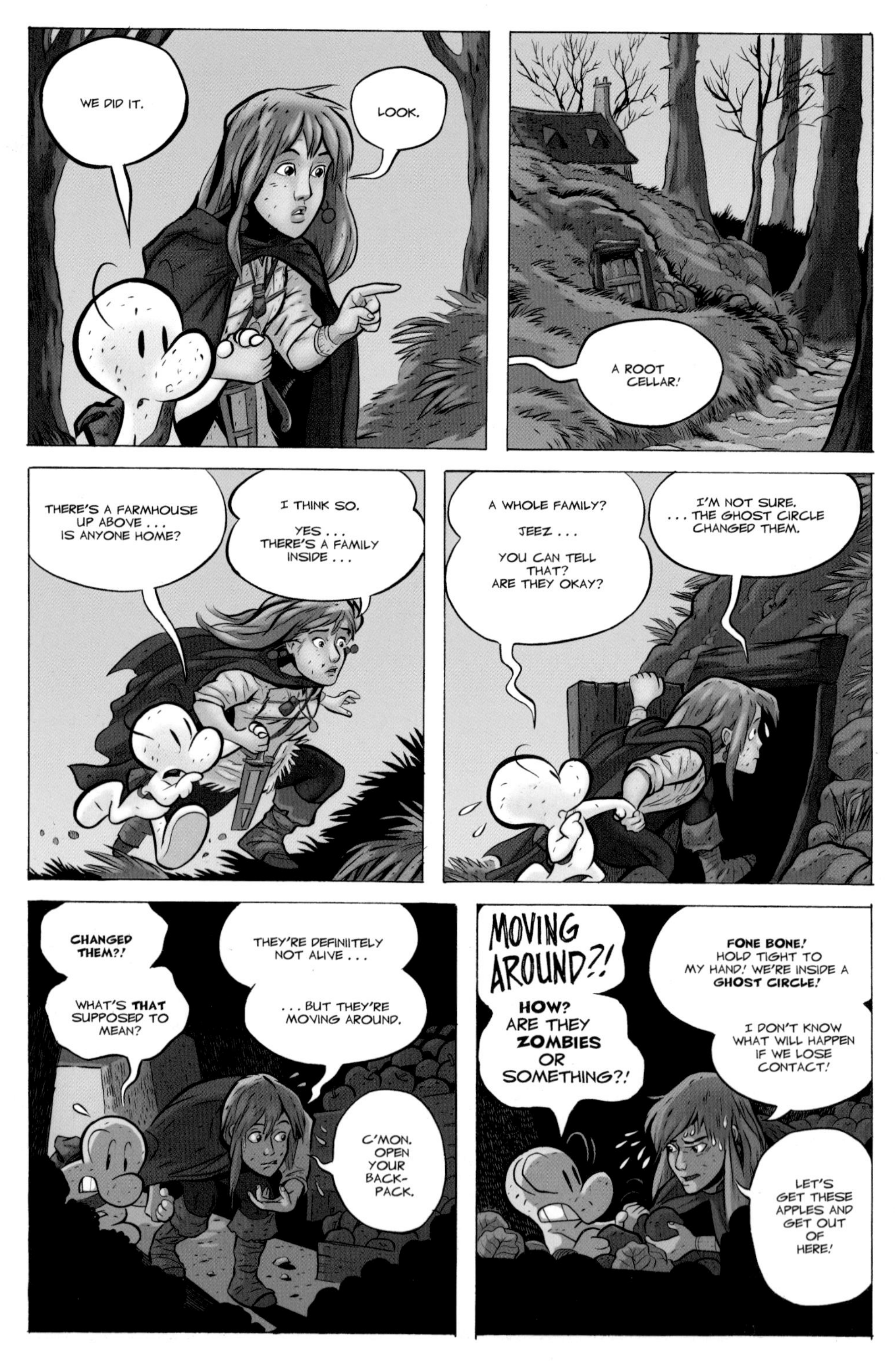
WE DID IT.
LOOK.
A ROOT CELLAR!
THERE'S A FARMHOUSE UP ABOVE . . . IS ANYONE HOME?
I THINK SO.
YES . . . THERE'S A FAMILY INSIDE . . .
A WHOLE FAMILY?
JEEZ . . .
YOU CAN TELL THAT? ARE THEY OKAY?
I'M NOT SURE. . . . THE GHOST CIRCLE CHANGED THEM.
CHANGED THEM?!
WHAT'S THAT SUPPOSED TO MEAN?
THEY'RE DEFINIITELY NOT ALIVE . . .
. . . BUT THEY'RE MOVING AROUND.
C'MON. OPEN YOUR BACK-PACK.
MOVING AROUND?!
HOW? ARE THEY ZOMBIES OR SOMETHING?!
FONE BONE! HOLD TIGHT TO MY HAND! WE'RE INSIDE A GHOST CIRCLE!
I DON'T KNOW WHAT WILL HAPPEN IF WE LOSE CONTACT!
LET'S GET THESE APPLES AND GET OUT OF HERE!

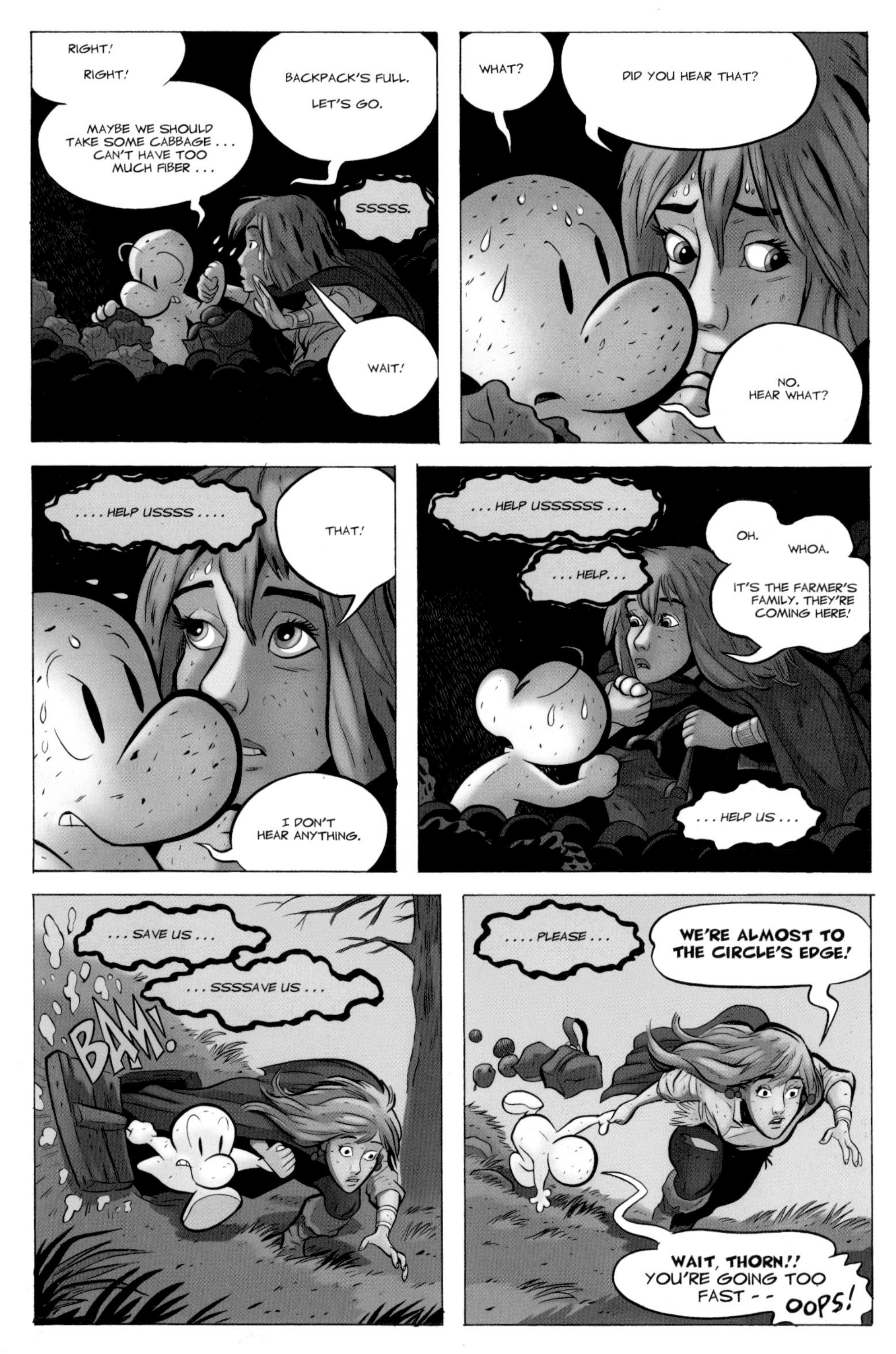
RIGHT!
RIGHT!
MAYBE WE SHOULD TAKE SOME CABBAGE . . . CAN'T HAVE TOO MUCH FIBER . . .
BACKPACK'S FULL. LET'S GO.
SSSSS.
WAIT!
WHAT?
DID YOU HEAR THAT?
NO. HEAR WHAT?
. . . . HELP USSSS . . . .
THAT!
I DON'T HEAR ANYTHING.
. . . HELP USSSSSS . . .
. . . HELP . . .
OH.
WHOA.
IT'S THE FARMER'S FAMILY. THEY'RE COMING HERE!
. . . HELP US . . .
. . . SAVE US . . .
. . . SSSSAVE US . . .
BAM!
. . . . PLEASE . . .
WE'RE ALMOST TO THE CIRCLE'S EDGE!
WAIT, THORN!! YOU'RE GOING TOO FAST - - OOPS!

I'M SORRY!
PAIN.
PAIN.
PRINCESSSSS . . .
HELP.
PRINCESS THORN . . .
WHERE ARE THEY?
THEY STOPPED BEHIND THE RIDGE.
HELP US, PRINCESS . . .
WHO ARE YOU?! WHAT DO YOU WANT?
FARMERS . . .
POOR FARMERS . .
HURT.
WHO'S HURT? ARE YOU HURT?
PRINCESS.
HELP.
PAIN.
STUBB.
STUBB? IS THAT YOUR NAME? FARMER STUBB?
YOUR MOTHER SENDS . . .
. . . A . . . MESSAGE . . .
MY MOTHER - - ?
MY MOTHER'S DEAD.
. . . SEEK THE CROWN OF HORNS . . .
CROWN OF HORNS. . . .
. . . PRINCESS . . .
PAIN.
HELP US.

WAIT! ARE YOU LEAVING?
FARMER STUBB?
HELLO?
WHAT ARE THEY SAYING?
NOTHING. I THINK THEY'RE GONE.
DANGER APPROACHES.
THE LOCUST SEEKS HIS MISSING PIECES.
PUT AWAY YOUR SWORD . . .
WEAPONS ATTRACT HIM.
YOU AND YOUR FRIEND . . .
IN GREAT DANGER . . .
WHAT SHOULD WE DO?
TAKE PIECE OF LOCUST BACK FROM YOUR FRIEND . . .
LEAVE THE GHOST CIRCLE.
NOW.
WHAT'S GOIN ON?
WE HAVE TO GET OUT OF HERE.
GIVE ME YOUR OTHER HAND FOR A MOMENT.
WHY?
NEVERMIND. JUST DO IT - - READY?
STEP - - !

WE'RE OUT!
uuuh...
THORN? ARE YOU OKAY?
OH . . . YEAH.
I'M GOOD.

YOU CAN GO IN, TINSMITH, BUT THE REST OF THE FARMERS WILL HAVE TO WAIT OUT HERE.
HELLO, LUCIUS.
HOW'S THE LEG?
MM.
CAN'T PUT ANY WEIGHT ON IT...
...BUT I CAN MANAGE WITH A CRUTCH.
IT'S NOT GOING WELL WITH THE HEADMASTER. HE REFUSES TO MOVE THE CAMP.
WHAT ABOUT THE VILLAGERS? WILL THEY GO SOUTH? JOINING THE ATHEIANS IS THE ONLY WAY TO **SURVIVE.**

THEY'LL DO WHATEVER YOU SAY, LUCIUS, BUT THE STICK-EATERS ARE WATCHING OUR EVERY MOVE. THEY'RE STARTING TO TREAT US LIKE PRISONERS.
STUPID HOLY MEN. CAN'T SEE PAST THEIR OWN HOODS.
THEY SAY THEY WANT TO PRESERVE THE VENI-YAN WAY OF LIFE.
FOR WHO?
WE'LL ALL BE DEAD WHEN THE LOCUST GETS HERE.
LISTEN . . .
THERE'S SOMETHING I HAVE TO ASK YOU ABOUT . . .
WHAT'S STOPPIN' YOU?
ON THE EVE OF THE BATTLE, THE HEADMASTER STARTED GRILLING ME ABOUT YOUR PAST. . . SAID YOU WERE SOME KIND OF SOLDIER.
YEAH, SO?
FIRST HE QUESTIONED YOUR LOYALTIES TO THE ORDER . . .
THEN HE SUGGESTED YOU WERE INDISCREET WHEN IT CAME TO THE ROYAL SISTERS.
JON OAKS - - I'M SORRY, LUCIUS, I KNOW HE WAS LIKE A SON TO YOU, MAY HE REST IN PEACE - - BUT HE SAID HE SAW THE LEADER OF THE RAT CREATURES, AND IT WAS ROSE BEN'S SISTER, BRIAR . . .
. . . AN' YOU WERE IN HER ARMS.
ANY CONNECTION BETWEEN THOSE TWO STORIES?

YEAH, THERE'S A CONNECTION.
THE HOODED ONE IS ROSE'S SISTER. BUT I DIDN'T KNOW THAT BEFORE THE BATTLE.
AND YES, I WAS A PALACE GUARD, SPENDING MY DAYS WITH TWO OF THE MOST BEWITCHING WOMEN I EVER MET.
I KNEW I SHOULDN'T GET INVOLVED WITH THEM . . .
BUT BLOODY STARS! YOU'D HAVE TO BE A PRIEST TO BE DISCREET AT THAT AGE.
ROSE WAS BEAUTIFUL AND KIND. . . I WAS IN LOVE WITH HER.
BUT BRIAR SEEMED MORE GROWN UP - -
IN WOMEN'S WAYS, IF YOU KNOW WHAT I MEAN.
AS USUAL . . .
SKRITCH
I PICKED THE WRONG ONE.
hmmp.
THAT WAS A LONG TIME AGO.

WENDELL?
I - - -
I HATE THIS WAR.
YOU KNOW MY BEST FRIEND EUCLID . . . WELL, I HAVEN'T BEEN ABLE TO FIND HIM SINCE THE VOLCANO ERUPTED.
I'M SORRY, LUCIUS . . .
I . . .
GET THE VILLAGERS TOGETHER.
WE'RE LEAVING.

CRUNCH
MUNCH!
THE FIRST TIME I RAN AWAY WAS WHEN I GOT MY TAIL CUT OFF.
REALLY? RAT CREATURES HAVE TAILS?
YES! WE'RE BORN WITH LONG, BEAUTIFUL HAIRLESS TAILS! BUT ONCE A YEAR, ON TAIL-CUTTING-OFF DAY, ALL THE ONE YEAR OLDS GET THEIR TAILS CHOPPED OFF.
WHAT IN THE WORLD FOR?
BECAUSE IF WE DON'T, THE JEKK WILL COME IN THE MIDDLE OF THE NIGHT AND DRAG US AWAY BY OUR TAILS!
YOU GOTTA BE KIDDING. A BUNCH OF MONSTERS WHO BELIEVE IN A BOOGIE MAN? WHAT'S TH' POINT?
DON'T LISTEN TO HIM, BARTLEBY! I'M SCARED OF MONSTERS, TOO! SOMETIMES I SLEEP WITH A LIGHT ON.
WE'RE ALSO SUPPOSED TO GET OUR EARS CROPPED, BUT I RAN AWAY BEFORE THEY COULD DO THAT.
SO WHAT HAPPENED WHEN YOU WENT BACK?

CRUNCH MUNCH!
NOBODY LIKED ME. THEY SAID I SPENT TOO MUCH TIME WITH YOU GUYS, AND I WOULDN'T EAT YOU WHEN THE TIME CAME . . .
THORN!

. . . I GUESS THEY WERE RIGHT.

GRAN'MA!
I... FEEL... SICK...

HONEY, WHAT'S WRONG?
I'LL BE ALL RIGHT.
HANG ON, THORN. WE'RE ALMOST THERE.
WHERE?

THE ONE PLACE IN ALL THE VALLEY THAT HASN'T SUCCUMBED TO THE GHOST CIRCLES.

TANEN GARD... SACRED BURIAL GROUND OF THE DRAGONS.
NO WAY.
ONCE WE PASS THROUGH THAT GORGE, I KNOW PEOPLE IN ATHEIA THAT CAN HELP THORN.
THEN WHAT ARE WE WAITING FOR? LET'S GO!

THERE'S A CATCH . . .
AFTER WHAT WE'VE BEEN THROUGH, WHAT COULD IT POSSIBLY **MATTER** IF THERE'S A CATCH?

IT'S FORBIDDEN FOR ANYONE OTHER THAN A DRAGON TO SET FOOT IN TANEN GARD.
THE PENALTY FOR TRESPASSING IS DEATH.

OH.

BONE
uuuhn...
THORN IS REALLY SICK, GRAN'MA - -
I DON'T THINK SHE CAN GO ON.
SHE **HAS** TO, BONE.
JUST TO THE CITY WALLS . . . ONCE WE REACH ATHEIA SHE CAN GET HELP.

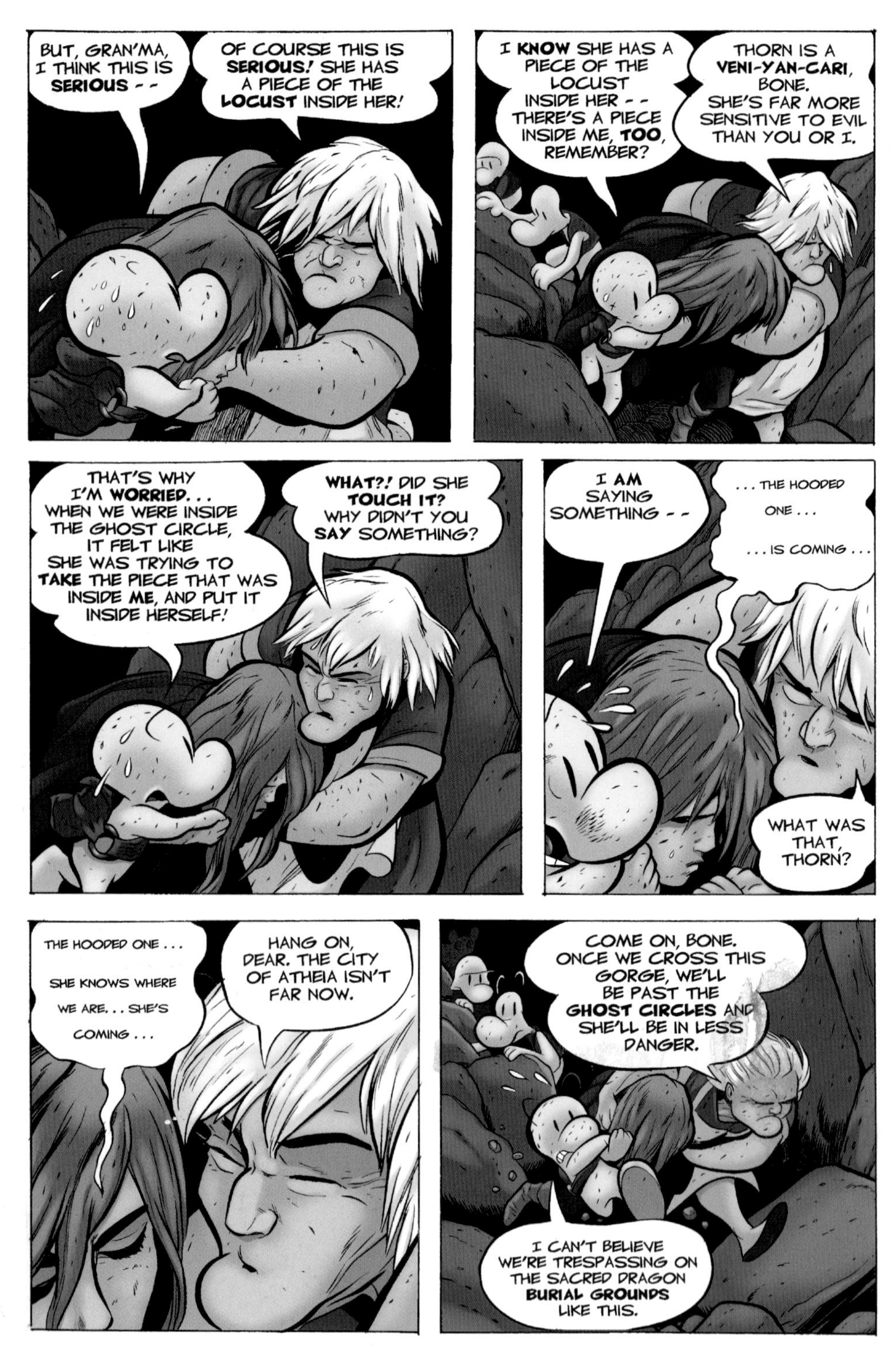
BUT, GRAN'MA, I THINK THIS IS SERIOUS - -
OF COURSE THIS IS SERIOUS! SHE HAS A PIECE OF THE LOCUST INSIDE HER!
I KNOW SHE HAS A PIECE OF THE LOCUST INSIDE HER - - THERE'S A PIECE INSIDE ME, TOO, REMEMBER?
THORN IS A VENI-YAN-CARI, BONE. SHE'S FAR MORE SENSITIVE TO EVIL THAN YOU OR I.
THAT'S WHY I'M WORRIED... WHEN WE WERE INSIDE THE GHOST CIRCLE, IT FELT LIKE SHE WAS TRYING TO TAKE THE PIECE THAT WAS INSIDE ME, AND PUT IT INSIDE HERSELF!
WHAT?! DID SHE TOUCH IT? WHY DIDN'T YOU SAY SOMETHING?
I AM SAYING SOMETHING - -
... THE HOODED ONE ...
... IS COMING ...
WHAT WAS THAT, THORN?
THE HOODED ONE ...
SHE KNOWS WHERE WE ARE... SHE'S COMING ...
HANG ON, DEAR. THE CITY OF ATHEIA ISN'T FAR NOW.
COME ON, BONE. ONCE WE CROSS THIS GORGE, WE'LL BE PAST THE GHOST CIRCLES AND SHE'LL BE IN LESS DANGER.
I CAN'T BELIEVE WE'RE TRESPASSING ON THE SACRED DRAGON BURIAL GROUNDS LIKE THIS.

HOW FAR ACROSS IS THE GORGE?
NOT FAR. I JUST HOPE THE LEGENDS ABOUT HOW DEEP IT IS ARE EXAGGERATED.
HOW DEEP IS IT SUPPOSED TO BE?
BOTTOMLESS.

BOTTOMLESS.
DIDN'T KNOW YOU COULD REALLY DO THAT.
ARE YOU SURE WE NEED TO CROSS?
ATHEIA IS ON THE OTHER SIDE.
UNLESS WE CAN FIND A WAY OVER, WE'RE TRAPPED.
PHONEY! SMILEY! COME ON!
YEAH, YEAH.
ERNF!
WE'RE COMIN'!

SMILEY! A LITTLE HELP!
SHHH! NOT SO LOUD, PHONEY! THE DRAGONS'LL HEAR!
I CAN'T REACH . . .
YOU REMEMBER WHEN WE WERE KIDS, AN' YOU USED TO MAKE ME STEAL FOOD FOR OUR MEALS?
WHAT'RE YOU TALKING ABOUT?
YOU MADE ME STEAL PIES OFF WINDOWSILLS BECAUSE I WAS THE TALLEST, REMEMBER? I ALWAYS WORRIED WE'D GET CAUGHT!
WE WERE ORPHANS. WE HAD TO GET OUR MEALS SOMEWHERE!
YOU WERE NEVER WORRIED THAT WE'D GET CAUGHT, REMEMBER THAT?
YEAH, I ALSO REMEMBER THAT ONCE I BECAME THE RICHEST BONE IN BONEVILLE, YOU MADE ME GO AROUND AND PAY EVERYONE BACK.
AND I'M VERY PROUD OF YOU FOR THAT, PHONEY. . .
BUT I STILL DON'T FEEL RIGHT.
WHAT'S THE MATTER? YOU AFRAID OF GETTING CAUGHT IN THE DRAGONS' GRAVEYARD?
I FEEL LIKE I'M PINCHIN' PIES OFF OL' LADY JOHNSON BONE'S WINDOWSILL!
WE SHOULDN'T BE HERE, IT'S DIS-RESPECT-FUL.

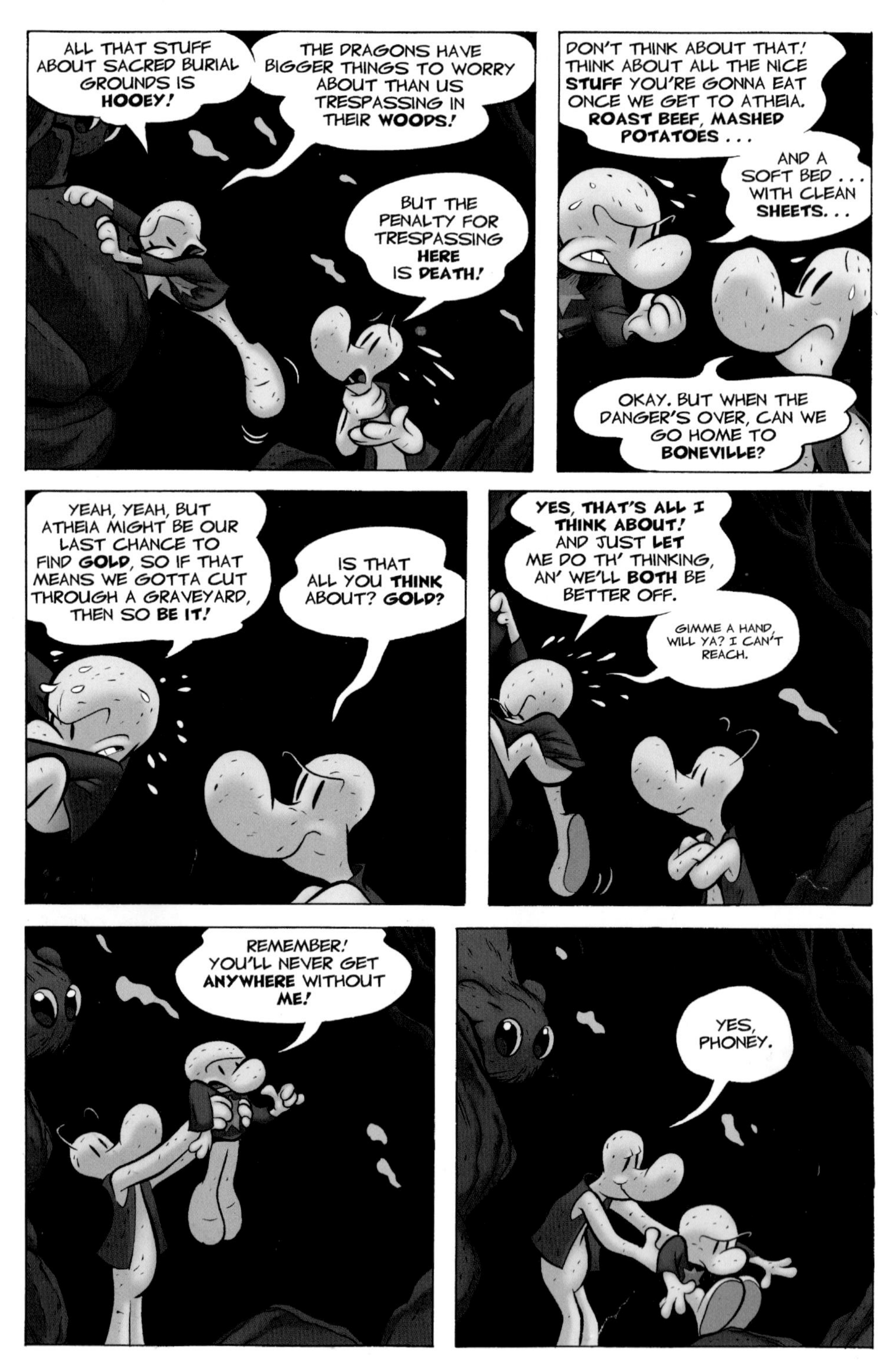
ALL THAT STUFF ABOUT SACRED BURIAL GROUNDS IS HOOEY!
THE DRAGONS HAVE BIGGER THINGS TO WORRY ABOUT THAN US TRESPASSING IN THEIR WOODS!
BUT THE PENALTY FOR TRESPASSING HERE IS DEATH!
DON'T THINK ABOUT THAT! THINK ABOUT ALL THE NICE STUFF YOU'RE GONNA EAT ONCE WE GET TO ATHEIA. ROAST BEEF, MASHED POTATOES . . .
AND A SOFT BED . . . WITH CLEAN SHEETS. . .
OKAY. BUT WHEN THE DANGER'S OVER, CAN WE GO HOME TO BONEVILLE?
YEAH, YEAH, BUT ATHEIA MIGHT BE OUR LAST CHANCE TO FIND GOLD, SO IF THAT MEANS WE GOTTA CUT THROUGH A GRAVEYARD, THEN SO BE IT!
IS THAT ALL YOU THINK ABOUT? GOLD?
YES, THAT'S ALL I THINK ABOUT! AND JUST LET ME DO TH' THINKING, AN' WE'LL BOTH BE BETTER OFF.
GIMME A HAND, WILL YA? I CAN'T REACH.
REMEMBER! YOU'LL NEVER GET ANYWHERE WITHOUT ME!
YES, PHONEY.

HEY, GUYS! LET'S GO!
WE FOUND A WAY ACROSS!
IT'S A BIG ROCK ARCH THAT'S REAL SKINNY AT THE TOP AND ABOUT A HUNDRED YARDS LONG.
IT'S PERFECT!
HEY!
DO YOU FEEL THAT? THE GROUND IS VIBRATING!
!
?
RRRRREEEEETKTK

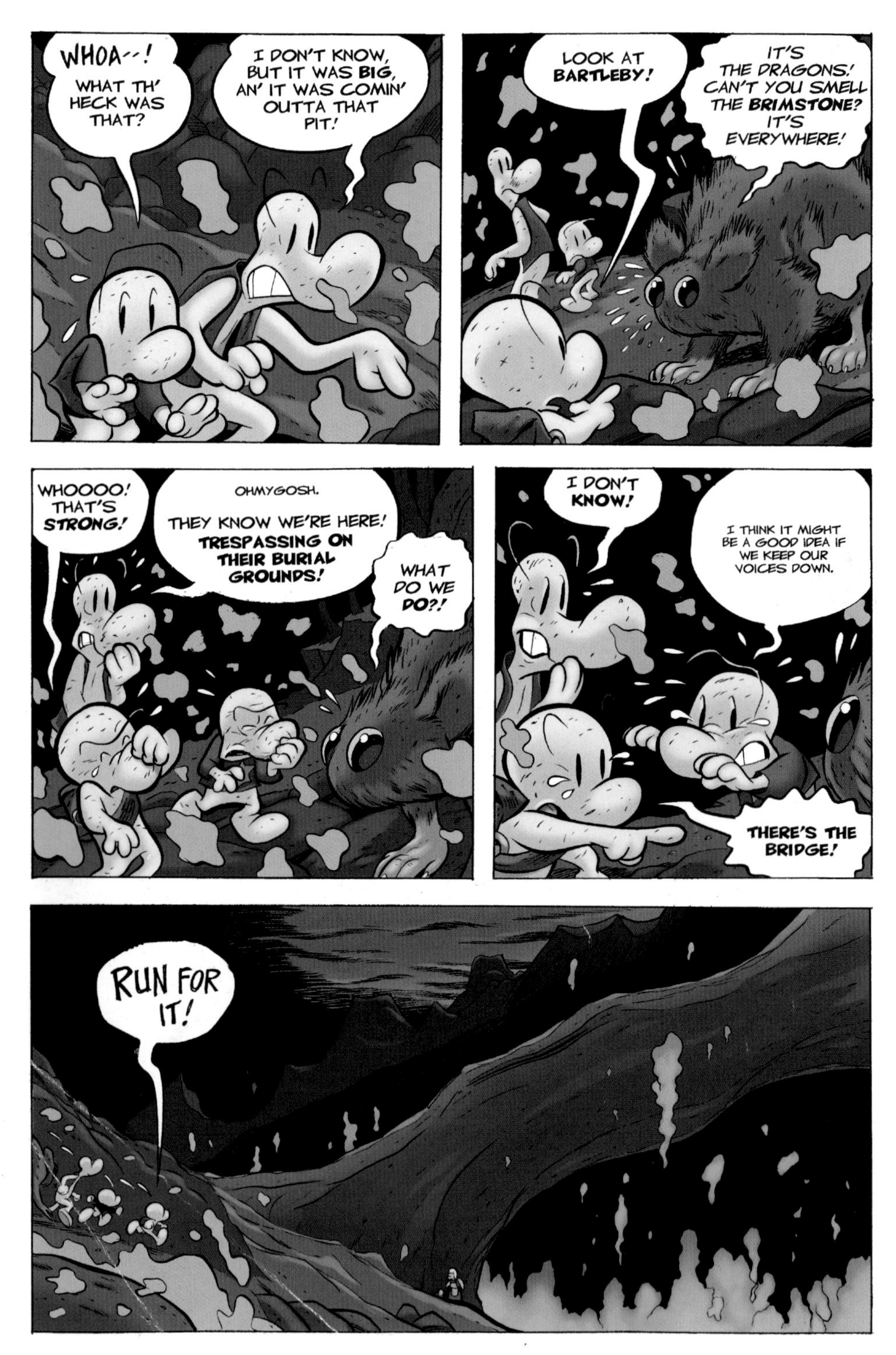
WHOA--! WHAT TH' HECK WAS THAT?
I DON'T KNOW, BUT IT WAS BIG, AN' IT WAS COMIN' OUTTA THAT PIT!
LOOK AT BARTLEBY!
IT'S THE DRAGONS! CAN'T YOU SMELL THE BRIMSTONE? IT'S EVERYWHERE!
WHOOOO! THAT'S STRONG!
OHMYGOSH.
THEY KNOW WE'RE HERE! TRESPASSING ON THEIR BURIAL GROUNDS!
WHAT DO WE DO?!
I DON'T KNOW!
I THINK IT MIGHT BE A GOOD IDEA IF WE KEEP OUR VOICES DOWN.
THERE'S THE BRIDGE!
RUN FOR IT!

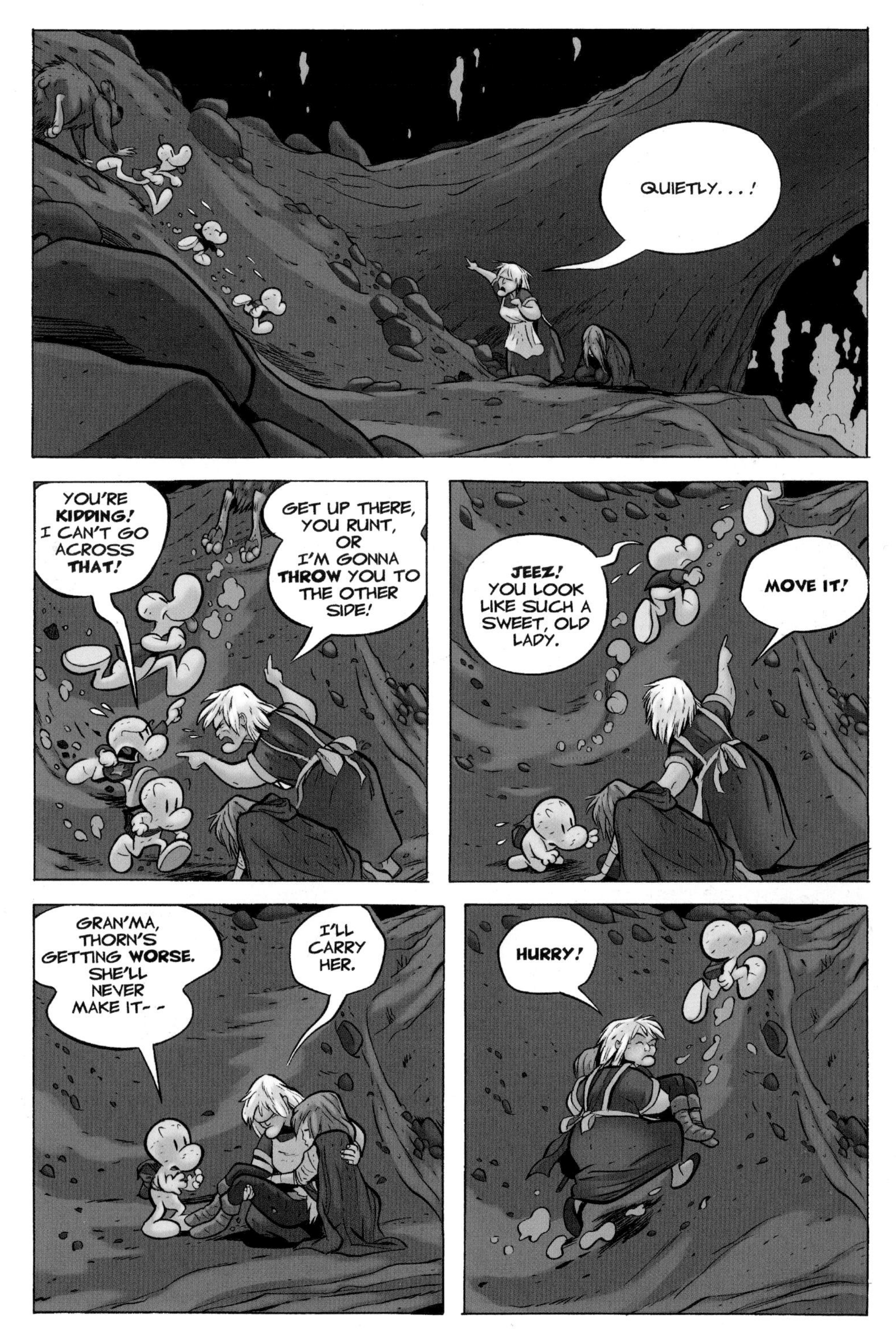
QUIETLY...!
YOU'RE KIDDING! I CAN'T GO ACROSS THAT!
GET UP THERE, YOU RUNT, OR I'M GONNA THROW YOU TO THE OTHER SIDE!
JEEZ! YOU LOOK LIKE SUCH A SWEET, OLD LADY.
MOVE IT!
GRAN'MA, THORN'S GETTING WORSE. SHE'LL NEVER MAKE IT- -
I'LL CARRY HER.
HURRY!

THIS IS
KINDA
SLIPPERY.
BE CAREFUL,
YOU GUYS...

WE'RE
GONNA
DIE.
QUIET!

SLIP!

uh,
oh..
FONE BONE!

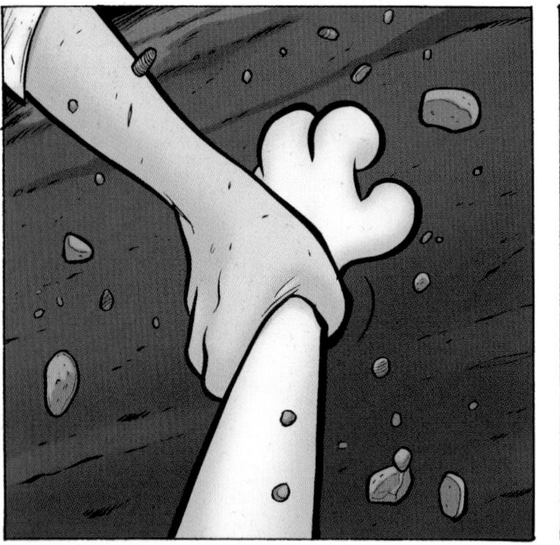

THORN! YOU'RE OKAY!
YES, I THINK I AM.

IN FACT, I FEEL REALLY GREAT!
HOW? WHAT HAPPENED?

IT'S THIS PLACE. SOMEHOW IT'S HEALING YOU.
YES, IT MAY BE.

COME! WE'RE ALMOST TO THE OTHER SIDE!

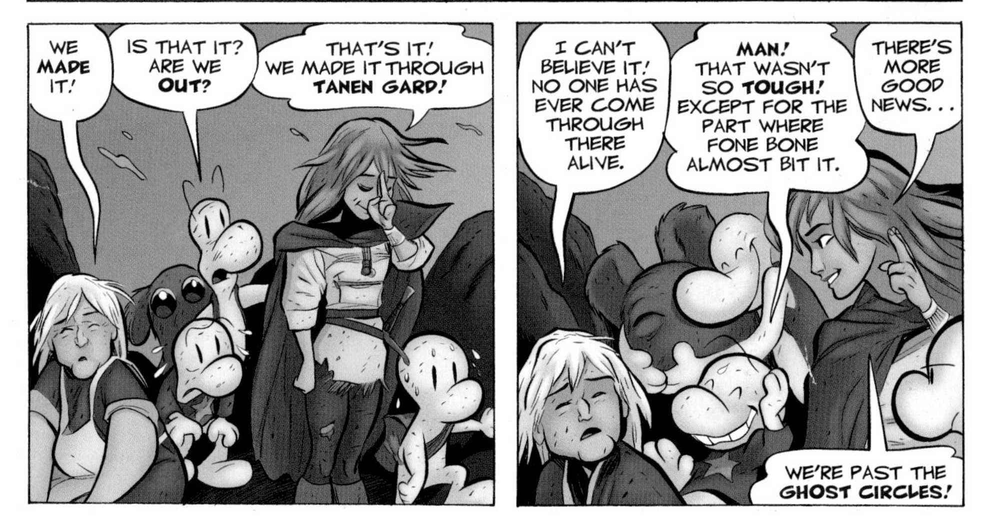
WE MADE IT!
IS THAT IT? ARE WE OUT?
THAT'S IT! WE MADE IT THROUGH TANEN GARD!
I CAN'T BELIEVE IT! NO ONE HAS EVER COME THROUGH THERE ALIVE.
MAN! THAT WASN'T SO TOUGH! EXCEPT FOR THE PART WHERE FONE BONE ALMOST BIT IT.
THERE'S MORE GOOD NEWS...
WE'RE PAST THE GHOST CIRCLES!

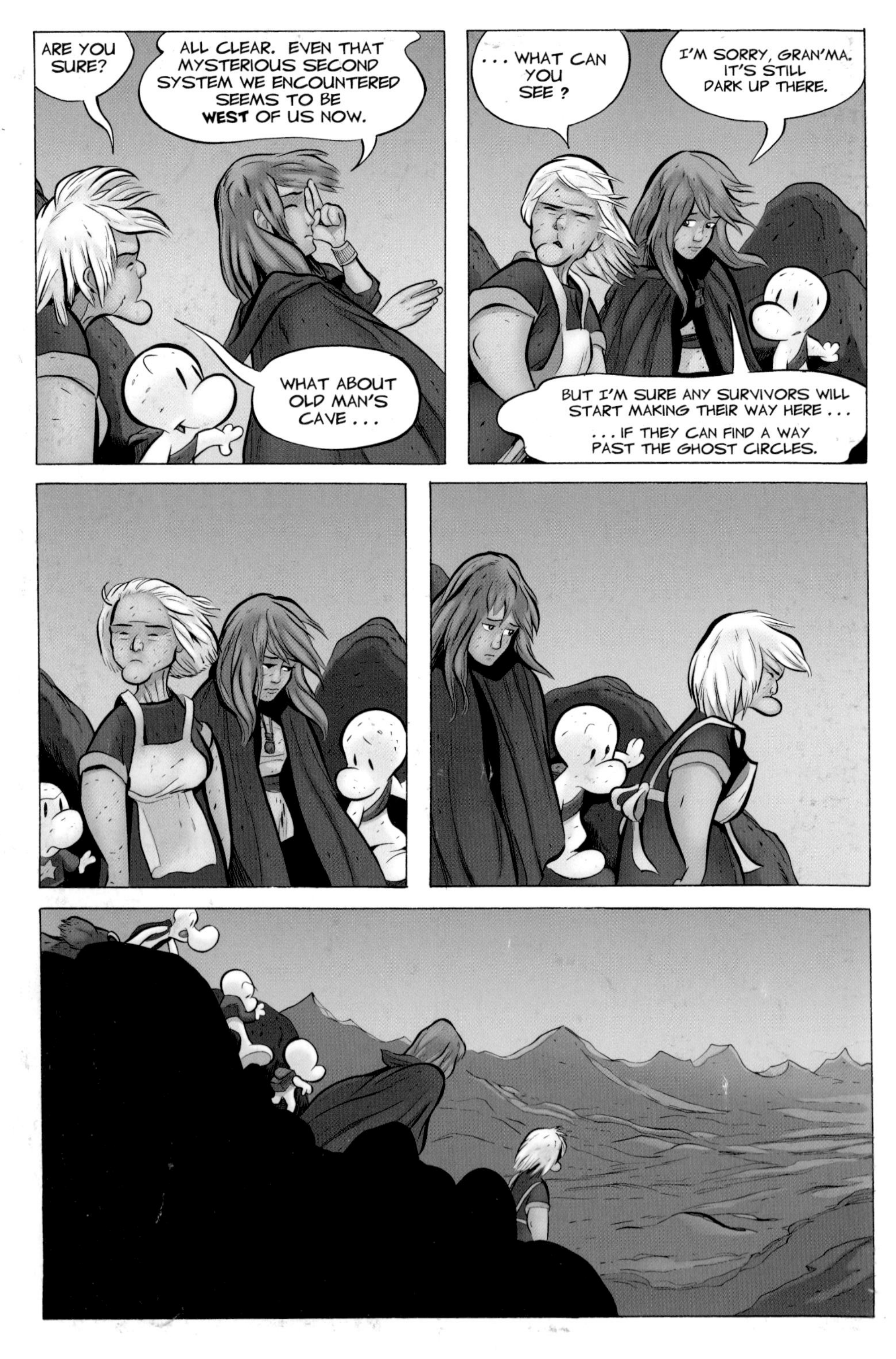
ARE YOU SURE?
ALL CLEAR. EVEN THAT MYSTERIOUS SECOND SYSTEM WE ENCOUNTERED SEEMS TO BE WEST OF US NOW.
WHAT ABOUT OLD MAN'S CAVE . . .
. . . WHAT CAN YOU SEE ?
I'M SORRY, GRAN'MA. IT'S STILL DARK UP THERE.
BUT I'M SURE ANY SURVIVORS WILL START MAKING THEIR WAY HERE . . .
. . . IF THEY CAN FIND A WAY PAST THE GHOST CIRCLES.

HALT!
DON'T COME ANY CLOSER!
YOU'RE THROUGH GIVIN' ORDERS AROUND HERE, STICK-EATER!
YEAH! WE WANT LUCIUS OUT OF THAT CELL NOW!!
I'LL CALL THE HEADMASTER - -
UURRK..
I'D STAND ASIDE IF I WERE YOU, SONNY BOY.
TAKE HIS SWORD.
YOU'RE MAKING A MISTAKE, LUCIUS. IT'S DANGEROUS OUT THERE!
SAVE IT FOR THE BROTHERHOOD.
EVERYBODY GOOD TO GO, WENDELL?
WOMEN AND CHILDREN ARE WAITING AT THE CREEK.
YOU GONNA BE OKAY ON THAT LEG?
GONNA HAVE TO BE.

ALL RIGHT, BOYS, LOOK ALIVE. WE'RE GOIN' OUT THE FRONT DOOR.
WHAT'S GOING ON HERE, LUCIUS? I GAVE ORDERS FOR YOU TO STAY IN YOUR CELL.
WE'RE LEAVING. WE'RE NOT ASKING YOU TO GO WITH US, BUT WE'RE LEAVING.
WHERE WOULD YOU GO? THE VALLEY HAS BEEN DESTROYED. OUT THERE IS DEATH . . .
HERE - - ONLY HERE HAS ANYTHING SURVIVED. WE HAVE FOOD AND SUPPLIES.
GATHER UP YOUR SUPPLIES AND COME WITH US! WE'LL GO SOUTH TO THE OLD KINGDOM. THERE MUST BE OTHER SURVIVORS!
NO.
THIS IS THE END OF THE WORLD AND WE ARE DISCIPLES OF VENU. IT IS OUR DUTY TO PROTECT THE VENI-YAN WAY OF LIFE!

ARE YOU **BLIND?** WE'RE GONNA **DIE** HERE!
WHY DON'T YOU TAKE OFF YOUR HOODS AND **SEE?!**
WHO CARES ABOUT PROTECTING YOUR SECRET BROTHERHOOD? WE'VE GOT **WIVES** AND **CHILDREN!**
IS THAT WHAT YOU WANT TO DO, HEADMASTER? PROTECT A SECRET BROTHERHOOD? AT THIS POINT, I HAVE TO ASK - -
WHO ARE YOU PROTECTING IT **FOR?**
WELL? WHAT'RE YOU GONNA DO? WE'RE IN A BIT OF A HURRY.
THE WORLD IS ENDING, REMEMBER?

GATHER THE SUPPLIES. WE WILL GO TO THE OLD KINGDOM TOGETHER.

PLIP
PLIP

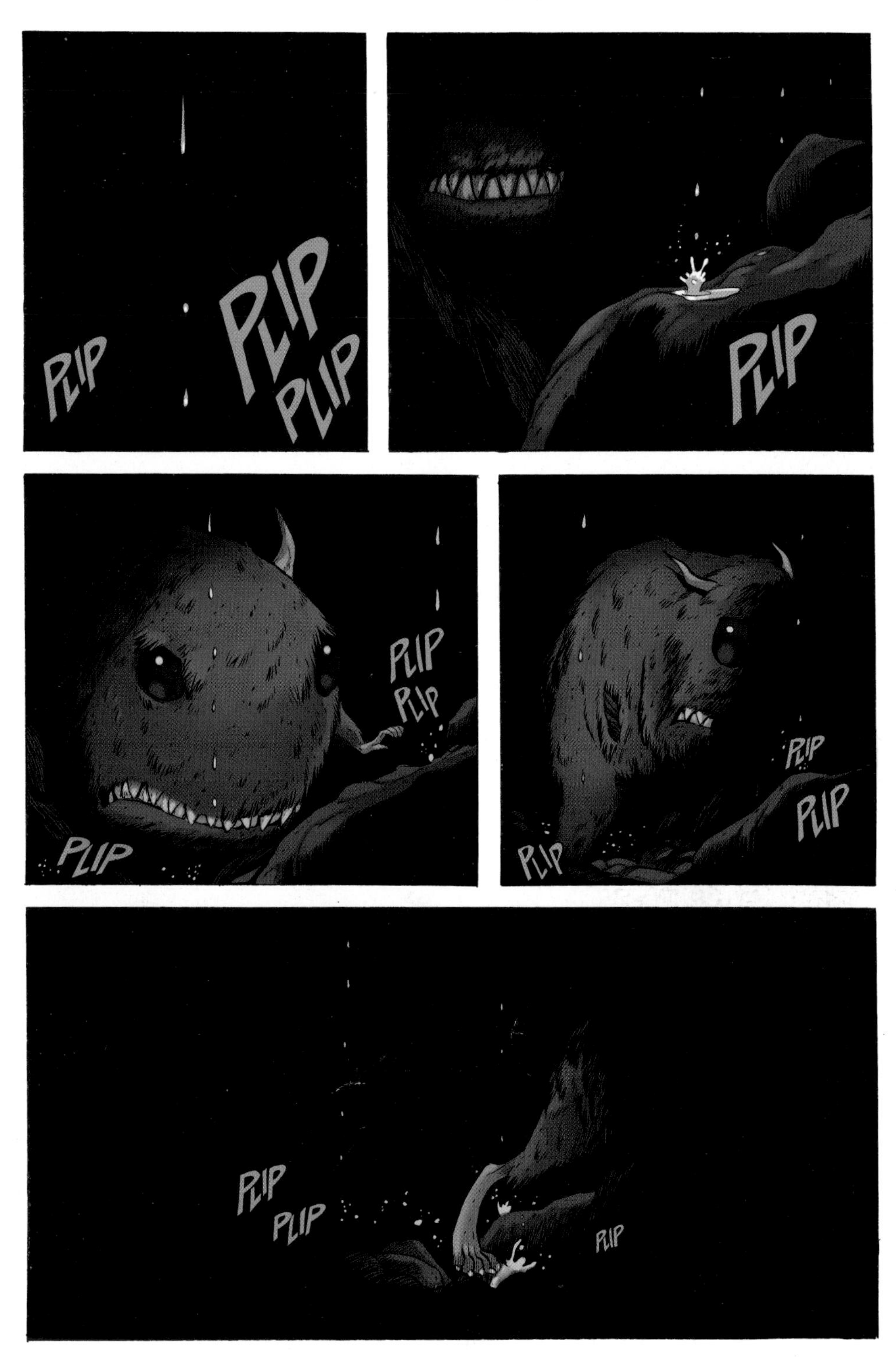
PLIP
PLIP
PLIP
PLIP
PLIP
PLIP
PLIP
PLIP
PLIP
PLIP
PLIP
PLIP
PLIP
PLIP

MORE CLIMBING?! AT LEAST THE GHOST CIRCLES WERE FLAT!
WE CAN GET A GOOD VIEW FROM UP HERE...
AND I WANT TO TAKE A LOOK AT THE ROAD THAT LEADS TO ATHEIA.
HEY-- ARE THOSE GRAVESTONES? I THOUGHT WE WERE OUT OF THE SACRED BURIAL GROUND.
WE ARE. THOSE ARE PRAYER STONES PUT HERE BY THE PEOPLE OF ATHEIA.
WHAT FOR? WHAT ARE PRAYER STONES?
ON THE STONE IS A PRAYER ASKING THE DRAGONS FOR BALANCE BETWEEN THE WORLD AND THE DREAMING.
THESE ARE THE BIG ONES...
...BUT AROUND THE NECK OF EVERY ATHEIAN, IN A SMALL POUCH, IS A SMALLER, PERSONAL PRAYER.

THE ONE YOU HAVE ON, THORN - - THAT BELONGED TO YOUR MOTHER. YOU WERE NEVER GIVEN ONE OF YOUR OWN BECAUSE UP NORTH THEY DON'T BELIEVE IN DRAGONS.
BUT DOWN HERE, THE DRAGONS ARE TREATED AS REPRESENTATIVES OF THE DREAMING.
CARVING THE PRAYER IN STONE GIVES IT STRENGTH AND PERMANENCE. . .
. . . AND BURYING IT IN THE GROUND DELIVERS IT STRAIGHT TO THE DRAGONS THEMSELVES.
YOU'RE GONNA LEAVE YOUR STONE BEHIND - - IN TH' DIRT?
I FIGURE ONE MORE GOOD PRAYER OUGHT TO BE ENOUGH FOR ME.
NOW THEN . . .
LET'S GET OUR BEARINGS, SHALL WE?

THAT'S THE PATH WE JUST CAME DOWN FROM THE BURIAL GROUND.
TANEN GARD IS PART OF THE SAME RIVER AND GORGE SYSTEM AS OLD MAN'S CAVE. THE RIVER RUNS ALL THE WAY UP THROUGH THE VALLEY BACK TO BARRELHAVEN.
TO THE SOUTH OF US LIES THE OLD PAWA-ATHEIA ROAD. THE CITY OF PAWA IS IN THE FOOTHILLS OF THE EASTERN MOUTAINS.
THE BRIDGE IS OUT. THE ROAD IS ABANDONED.
THE PAWANIANS HAVE GONE OVER TO THE LOCUST. TRADE BETWEEN THE TWO ANCIENT CITIES HAS CEASED.
THIS IS THE DIRECTION WE NEED TO GO.
WEST.
TWO DAYS WALK WILL BRING US TO WITHIN SIGHT OF ATHEIA'S GATES.
HMMM. THE GHOST CIRCLES WILL SLOW THE RAT CREATURES DOWN, BUT THAT'S STILL TWO DAYS OUT IN THE OPEN.

IT'S RISKY, BUT IT'S OUR BEST HOPE OF FINDING SANCTUARY AND MOUNTING A DEFENSE.
THE ROAD **SEEMS** DESERTED.
I STILL HAVEN'T LOCATED THE SOURCE OF THE SOUTHERN GHOST CIRCLES.
UNTIL WE FIND THAT SOURCE, THERE'S UNKNOWN DANGER EVEN HERE IN THE OLD KINGDOM.
THERE ALWAYS WAS.
JUST A LITTLE FARTHER, EVERYONE. WE'RE ALMOST THERE.
oh, BOY, oh, BOY! I CAN'T WAIT!
I BET TH' STREETS ARE PAVED WITH **GOLD!**
YOU'RE A FUNNY EGG, YOU KNOW THAT?

I'M A FUNNY EGG? **YOU'RE** A FUNNY EGG!
NO, I'M NOT!
WHAT AM I, BARTLEBY?
YOU'RE **ACES**, SMILEY!

...TO BE CONTINUED.

About JEFF SMITH

JEFF SMITH was born and raised in the American Midwest and learned about cartooning from comic strips, comic books, and watching animated shorts on TV. After four years of drawing comic strips for The Ohio State University's student newspaper and co-founding Character Builders animation studio in 1986, Smith launched the comic book *BONE* in 1991. Between *BONE* and other comics projects, Smith spends much of his time on the international guest circuit promoting comics and the art of graphic novels.

More about *BONE*

An instant classic when it first appeared in the U.S. as an underground comic book in 1991, *BONE* has since garnered 38 international awards and sold a million copies in 15 languages. Now, Scholastic's GRAPHIX imprint is publishing full-color graphic novel editions of the nine-book *BONE* series. Look for the continuing adventures of the Bone cousins in *Treasure Hunters*.